W9-BMX-369

The Paper Door

and Other Stories

Shiga Naoya

Translated by Lane Dunlop

For Norma Jean

Lane Dunlop

✲

NORTH POINT PRESS
San Francisco 1987

Printed in the United States of America
Library of Congress Catalogue Card Number: 86-60992
ISBN: 0-86547-260-2

Acknowledgments are due to the editors of the following magazines, in which these stories (some in slightly different form) first appeared: "The Razor" and "The Shopboy's God" in *New England Review and Bread Loaf Quarterly*; "At Kinosaki," "Infatuation," and "A Gray Moon" in *Prairie Schooner*; "The House by the Moat" in *The Literary Review*.

To the Memory of
Ivan Morris
my mentor
and
Sachiko Murakami
who taught me my first Japanese

Table of Contents

Translator's Preface

Shiga Naoya was born on February 20th, 1883, the second son of Shiga Naoharu and O-Gin. His father Naoharu was an employee of a branch of the Dai-Ichi Bank in the harbor town of Ishinomaki in Miyagi Prefecture at the time of Shiga's birth. Shiga's mother died of morning sickness in August, 1895, his father remarrying in the fall of the same year. Shiga has written movingly of his mother in an early story called "The Death of My Mother and the New Mother." In "The White Line," a piece written in his later years, Shiga says: ". . . I have no memory of the scent of my mother's body. What I can recall vividly even now, however, is the thick white line of the calves of my mother's legs. Tucking up the skirts of her kimono behind like a housemaid, exposing her white undergarments, my mother would swab down the veranda on her hands and knees."

Although Shiga got on well with his stepmother, his relations with his father gradually worsened from June, 1901, until their reconciliation in 1917. The occasion of their first clash was a recrudescence of the public controversy over the copper mines at Ashio in Tochigi Prefecture, in continuous operation since the early Tokugawa period. During the last fifteen years of the nineteenth century and the first twenty years of the twentieth, the deleterious effect of cupreous tailings on the miners and the farmers of the vicinity came up intermittently for debate in the Diet. Inspired by the debate raging anew just then, Shiga and a few like-minded friends determined to make an inspection trip to the locality in question. This was forbidden by his father, marking the first serious disagreement between them.

Three years later, at twenty-one, Shiga wrote his first story, "The Little Girl and the Rapeseed Flower," initiating the early period of his work (1904–1914). This story was written on a trip to Mt. Kano in Kazusa, while Shiga was in upper school. It antedates "As Far as Abashiri," although the latter was Shiga's first published story. Seven of the stories in this selection are from Shiga's early period: "The Little Girl and the Rapeseed Flower," "As Far As Abashiri," "The Razor," "The Paper Door," "Seibei and His Gourds," "An Incident," and "Han's Crime." Shiga's stories might be divided into three categories: those based on experience and observation, those that are faithful to ideal experience or imagination, and those that are more or less autobiographical. Thus, the second and the sixth of the stories listed above belong to the first category, the first, third, and seventh to the second category, and the fourth to the third category. It will be readily seen that there are overlaps: for instance, "Seibei and His Gourds" is autobiographical in its account of the son's resistance against a crass, overbearing father, and based on the ideal in its description of the boy's love of beauty. Imagination shapes reality in "The Razor," although the incident described is completely plausible. In "The Paper Door," both the "I" who records the friend's story and the friend himself are aspects of Shiga: the note of disgust at the end has the bite of self-disgust. And so on and so forth. During this early period, Shiga, increasingly at odds with his family, moved about a good deal. There were sojourns in Onomichi, Matsue, and Kyoto. Having left Tokyo University without taking a degree, and living at home with no fixed occupation until late in his twenties, Shiga was bound to incur much family displeasure. As the critic Takada Mizuho has remarked: "It was to be expected that his family, in particular his father, should feel profound uneasiness about a son who was so consistently true to himself."

In 1914, with Shiga's marriage against his father's wishes to

Kadenokoji Sadako, a cousin of the writer Mushanokoji Saneatsu, the break between them became total. Shiga removed his name from the family register—in other words, disinherited himself—and set up his own family. However, father and son were reconciled in 1917: the event is the subject of a famous novella-length account by Shiga entitled *Reconciliation* (*Wakai*). During these three years, Shiga wrote or at least published nothing at all. In addition to family turmoil, there was the failure of his ambitious autobiographical novel *Tokito Kensaku*. This work, done partly at the behest of his mentor, the celebrated novelist Natsume Soseki, was later to become *A Dark Night's Passing*, upon which much of Shiga's reputation rests. But its failure at the time apparently left Shiga unable to hold up his head before Soseki, his spiritual father, and it was not until the latter's death in 1916 that Shiga was able to write again.

This brings us to Shiga's middle period (1917–1927). The stories of this period included in this selection are "At Kinosaki," "Akanishi Kakita," "Incident on the Afternoon of November Third," "The Shopboy's God," "Rain Frogs," "The House by the Moat," "A Memory of Yamashina," "Infatuation," and "Kuniko." In "At Kinosaki," the clarity of insight is accompanied by calmness of feeling. This contrasts with earlier stories such as "Han's Crime" and "The Razor," in which excitement of feeling is the condition of the clarity of insight. In "Akanishi Kakita," there is a rather fatalistic acceptance of fate of a sort that we are accustomed to think of as Oriental. However, in the next story, "Incident on the Afternoon of November Third," there is a burning, although characteristically understated, hatred of the brutality of military training. "The Shopboy's God" is one of the reasons that Shiga became known as "the god of the short story." The critic Takada remarks that "its perfection and harmony have the immovable beauty of an old art object." The underlying theme of "Rain Frogs," which from evidence in the last book of *A Dark Night's Passing* would appear to have an autobiographical basis, is the avoidance of tragedy by the acceptance of one's fate. "The House by the Moat" may be read as a journal of Shiga's sojourn in Matsue, while "A Memory of Yamashina" and "Infatuation" are the first two of a series of four stories dealing with a crisis in Shiga's married life over his affair with a twenty-year-old tea house waitress, when he was in his early forties. Shiga has said of these stories that as a writer he was less interested in the affair itself than in its effects on his domestic arrangements.

In "Kuniko," Shiga is imagining what could have happened had he gone on with his love affairs. Its subject is the classic dilemma of the writer who finds that his search for experience may destroy not only his personal relationships but also the lives of others. At one point the narrator, a playwright chafing against the tedium of domestic harmony, remarks to his wife: "It sounds like a complaint, but if you'll allow me to say so, I feel as if this peaceful, uneventful life for the past several years has started to rot me, not that I'm a prize peach or anything. My life has gone bad—what I mean is I've lost the desire to write." In his solitary arguments with himself, he states the attitude of society: "For us, it is of no importance whether a playwright like yourself can or cannot create more than one woman character. Instead we should prefer you to avoid making your one woman the least bit unhappy on that account. Probably it will be as well for you to hatch goldfish eggs. The patching of paper doors, too, will be good. It is a good thing, also, to try to make the dahlias bloom beautifully." These passages would seem to reflect a crisis in Shiga's life, in which, in contrast to the outcome of the story, the humane person won out over the artist.

"Kuniko" marks the end of Shiga's middle period. It may be said that once he'd achieved the clarity of insight and resolution of conflict that he worked for in his stories, he felt free to turn to other forms. Although the writing of *A Dark Night's Passing* is dated 1921–1937, it was the reworking of material that already existed in the failed *Tokito Kensaku* (1912–1914). From "Kuniko" (1927) on, Shiga's eye turns outward and backward. The work of his late period (1928–1963) is comprised mainly of incidental pieces, reminiscences, miscellaneous essays, accounts of family activities, travel diaries, and the like. "A Gray Moon," a delicately observed minor incident, represents the style of his later years at its best.

In a late piece entitled "The Yatsude Flower," Shiga remarks rather disarmingly that he no longer wishes to write short stories, having grown weary of the disagreeable minutiae of people's lives. He now prefers to look at flowers. In "The White Line," he points out that his much-acclaimed early story "The Death of My Mother and the New Mother" is based on a misunderstanding, a failure to see beyond his own feelings. He now possesses the wisdom to see around a situation, rather than having to write his way through it. It is the real-life resolution of the crisis recorded in "Kuniko," the choice of life over art, that would seem to account for what amounts to a forty-five-year retirement from the art of short story writing. There is no reason to doubt that his family life during this period was full and happy. Apparently Shiga had it both ways: perfection of the work *and* the life. He died in 1971.

LANE DUNLOP

✲

✲

The Paper Door

✲

✲

The Little Girl and the Rapeseed Flower

✲

It was the afternoon of a quiet, bright spring day. A little girl was gathering kindling on the mountainside.

By and by, as the sun could be seen glowing crimson through the sparse new greenery of the trees, the little girl, after carrying the branches she'd gathered down to a small meadow, began to pack them into an open-work basket that she had brought with her on her back.

Suddenly, the little girl felt as if she were being called to by someone.

"Yes?" the little girl asked, despite herself. Standing up, she looked all around her. But there was no one to be seen.

"Who called me?" the little girl asked again, in a loud voice. But again there was no answer.

After she'd had this feeling two or three times, the little girl suddenly realized that the voice came from a little rapeseed flower that was all by itself, barely holding up its head in a patch of weeds.

Wiping her face with the cloth she wore around her head, the little girl said:

"I would have thought you'd be lonely in a place like this."

"I *am* lonely," the flower answered in an intimate voice.

"Then why did you come here?" the little girl asked, reprovingly.

"A seed got stuck in the breast down of a skylark and fell off here. I don't know what to do," said the flower sadly. Then it asked the little girl to take it with her down to the village at the foot of the mountain, where there were many of its kind.

The little girl felt sorry for the rapeseed flower. She decided to grant its wish. Gently disengaging it from the soil and carrying it in her cupped hand, she went down the mountain road toward the village.

Alongside the road, making the sounds of water, a clear little brook flowed. Time passed. "Your hand is awfully warm," the rapeseed flower said. "My head feels heavy, and I just can't hold it up straight." At each step the little girl took, it weakly nodded its drooping head.

For a moment, the little girl didn't know what to do.

Then, unexpectedly, she had a good idea. Quickly squatting by the roadside, she silently dipped the roots of the rapeseed flower in the water.

"Maa!" exclaimed the flower, in a revived, lively voice. It looked up at the little girl. Whereupon, as if handing down a verdict, the little girl said:

"From here on, you travel by water."

Shaking its head uneasily, the rapeseed flower said:

"If I'm carried on ahead of you, I'll be frightened."

"There's nothing to be afraid of." And with that the little girl suddenly let go of the flower.

"I'm afraid, I'm afraid!"

Immediately swept off by the current, the rapeseed flower shrieked with terror as it was carried farther and farther away from the little girl. But the little girl didn't answer a word. Putting her hands behind her, holding up the basket that danced on her back, she came running after.

The rapeseed flower breathed a sigh of relief. Then, looking up joyfully from the water's surface, it talked with the little girl about this and that.

From somewhere, a butterfly came fluttering buoyantly. Annoyingly, it bobbed and danced all around the rapeseed flower's head. The rapeseed flower was even happy about that. But then the busy, fickle butterfly flew away somewhere else.

Noticing that beads of sweat, like jewels, were forming at the tip of the little girl's nose, the rapeseed flower said in a worried voice:

"Now it's you who are having a hard time." But the little girl replied somewhat shortly:

"Don't worry about me."

Thinking it had been scolded, the rapeseed flower was silent.

A moment later, the little girl was startled by a shriek from the rapeseed flower. Its roots entangled in some water weeds that undulated in the current like long hair, the rapeseed flower waved its head back and forth in great distress.

"Well now. Just rest there for a minute." Out of breath, the little girl sat down on a rock by the side of the brook.

"How can I rest with my feet caught like this? I feel so uncomfortable." The rapeseed flower voiced its complaint more and more earnestly.

"You're all right that way," the little girl replied.

"I'm *not* all right. It's good to rest, but when it's like this it's just awful. Please, lift me out. Please," begged the rapeseed flower. But the little girl, smiling and saying "You're all right," would not listen.

Soon, though, by the force of the current, the rapeseed flower's roots slipped loose by themselves. With a sudden, sharp cry of "I'm being carried away!" the rapeseed flower was once again borne away downstream. Jumping up, the little girl ran after it.

After they'd gone a short distance, the rapeseed flower said timidly:

"You *are* having a hard time."

"It's nothing," the little girl answered gently. Then, so the rapeseed flower wouldn't feel anxious, she decided to run on ahead by fifteen feet or so.

The village at the foot of the mountain came into view. The little girl called out: "It won't be long now."

"That's right," the rapeseed flower answered behind her.

For a while, neither said anything. The only sounds were the *pata-pata, pata-pata* of the little girl's straw sandals as she ran, mingling with the gurgling of the brook.

"*Cha-pon*!" At the little girl's feet, there was a sudden splashing sound. The rapeseed flower let out a shriek as if it were about to die. Startled, the little girl stopped and looked back. Its petals and leaves pale with fear, reaching up from the surface, the rapeseed flower screamed: "Quick! Quick!" Hastily, the little girl took it out of the water.

"What's the matter?" Cradling the rapeseed flower against her breast, the little girl looked behind them at the stream.

"Something jumped in from by your feet." Palpitating, the rapeseed flower spoke in fits and starts.

"It was a wart-frog. He went under once, and then all of a sudden came up right in front of me. Another inch, and our cheeks would have bumped together. He had a pointy mouth and looked all grouchy like a river imp," the rapeseed flower said. The little girl gave a loud laugh.

"It's not funny," the rapeseed flower said, in a reproachful voice. "But then, when I screamed, it was the wart-frog who was surprised. He dove under in a panic." Saying this, the rapeseed flower also laughed.

Before long, they came to the village.

The little girl immediately replanted the rapeseed flower in the field behind her house.

There, unlike the weedy slope of the mountain, the soil was rich.

The rapeseed flower grew up rapidly.

And there, among many friends and companions of its own kind, it lived happily ever after.

✲

✲

As Far As Abashiri

✲

A friend in Utsunomiya, to whom I'd said, "I'll stop by your place on my way back from Nikko," had replied, "Invite me along—I'll go to Nikko with you."

It was terribly hot, even for August. Selecting the 4:20 afternoon train, I planned to get off at the station near my friend's place. The train was bound for Aomori. When I got to Ueno Station, a crowd of people had gathered outside the ticket gate. I immediately joined them.

A bell rang, and the gate opened. All at once people stirred and stood up. The nonstop sound of a ticket punch started up. People grimacing as they tugged at their luggage caught between the railings, people pushed out of the mainstream and frantically attempting to get back in, people not about to let them—it was the usual mob scene. A policeman, standing behind the ticket taker, hostilely eyed the passengers one by one. Those who had finally made it through hurried out onto the platform with quick little steps. Ignoring the porters' calls of "Empty seats up ahead, empty seats up ahead," they swarmed aboard the nearest cars. Meaning to ride on the most forward car, I hurried on ahead.

Sure enough, the forward cars were empty. I boarded the last compartment of the first car. People who'd been unable to find seats in the rear cars slowly came milling toward this one. But there was room for only about three-fourths of them. It was almost departure time. Rear and front, there was the sound of doors being closed, the clicking of catches. A redcap, about to close the door of my compartment, raised his hand.

"In here, madam. In here." He opened the door again and waited. A pale, thin-haired woman of twenty-six or -seven, with a baby on her back and leading a boy by the hand, came inside. The train was under way.

The woman sat down on the far side, by the window where the setting sun shone in. It was the only seat left.

"Mother. Out of the way." The boy, about seven, frowned as he spoke.

"It's hot there." Putting the baby down, the mother spoke quietly.

"I like it hot."

"If you're in the sunlight, your underwear will itch."

"So?" Making a devil's face, the boy glared at his mother.

"Taki." The mother put her face close to the boy's. "We're going on a long trip now. If your underwear starts to itch on the way, Mother won't know what to do and will really feel like crying. You're a good boy. Please listen to what Mother says. Before long, there'll be a seat out of the sunlight. As soon as there is, you'll sit there. Do you understand?"

"I have an awful headache," the child went on, intent on getting his way. A sad look came over the mother's face.

"Mother just doesn't know what to do."

Suddenly, I said:

"Sit over here." I made a little space by the window. "It's out of the sun."

The boy looked at me with unfriendly eyes. A funny sort of pasty-faced, flat-headed brat, I thought. He gave me the creeps. The child had cotton stuffed in his nostrils and ears.

"Oh, how kind of you." The mother, a smile coming into her sad face, put her hand to the boy's back as though to push him toward me. "Taki, say thank you. Sit where the gentleman says."

"Come on." Taking the boy's hand, I made him sit next to me. The boy, with an odd look, glanced at me now and then, but after a while he fixed his eyes on the passing scenery.

"Try to look only that way. Otherwise cinders will get in your eye."

Even when I said this, the boy didn't answer. By and by, we came to Uruwa. Here the two people sitting across from me got off. The mother moved into their places with her luggage. I say "luggage," but it was only a cloth bag of the kind women use and a kerchief bundle.

"Now, Taki, sit over here. Thank you so much, sir." The mother politely bowed her head to me. The baby, until now lulled asleep by the train's movement, woke up and started to cry.

"Never mind, never mind." Cradling and rocking the baby on her lap, the mother tried to soothe it. "Chi-chi-ka, chi-chi-ka." But the baby, flat on its back with legs outspread, cried more and more. "Oh, never mind, never mind," the mother said again, and then: "I have something good for you." Reaching out with one hand, she took out a "Garden Dew" drop from the cloth bag. But even that didn't stop the baby's crying. At her side, the boy, looking very discontented, said:

"Mother. What about me?"

"Take one out for yourself." Opening her kimono, the mother gave the baby her breast. Taking a slightly soiled silk handkerchief from her obi, she tucked it in at her throat to cover her naked bosom.

The boy, plunging his hand into the cloth bag, groped around in it.

"Hey. These aren't the right ones." He shook his head.

"They aren't? What kind do you want?"

" 'Jewels.' "

"There aren't any 'Jewels.' I didn't bring any."

"That stinks! It stinks if there aren't any 'Jewels,' " the boy whined through his nose.

"There are some others at the bottom. Take them. Be a good boy, now. Those ones are delicious, too."

The boy nodded reluctantly. Again with one hand, the mother took out four drops or so and placed them in the boy's hand.

"More." The mother added two more.

Satiated with milk, the baby started twiddling a black-spotted tortoiseshell comb that had fallen out of the mother's hair. It ended by trying to cram the comb into its mouth.

"Mustn't do that." As the mother held back its tiny hand, the baby, mouth open, turned its face that way. Two minuscule white teeth were visible in its lower gum.

"Yes. Good, good," cooed the mother, holding a "Garden Dew" drop, which had fallen into her lap, in front of the baby's face. The baby, who'd been gurgling "aa, aa," silently gazed cross-eyed at it. Letting go of the comb, it grasped the drop in its chubby fist. Then, fist and all, it tried to stuff the drop into its mouth. Strings of drool hung down from its mouth.

Half laying the baby on its side, the mother felt between its thighs. Evidently it was wet there.

"I'll have to change diapers," the mother said, as if to herself. Then, to the boy:

"Taki. Let me have your seat a moment. I have to change baby's diaper."

"Oh, no! I don't like this, Mother." Scowling, the boy got up.

"Sit over here." Once again, I cleared the space where I had had him sit before.

"It's extremely kind of you. He's being very difficult. I don't know what to do when he's this way." The mother gave me a lonely smile.

"Probably it's because of his nose and ears."

"Excuse me." Turning around, the mother took out a dry diaper and some oilpaper to wrap up the wet one.

"It is just as you say."

"How long have they been that way?"

"Ever since he was born. The doctor said it's because the father drinks too much, but I wonder if his head isn't bad."

The baby, tumbled face up on the seat, stared unseeingly at nothing. Waving its hands, it gave voice. "Aa, aaa." Quickly changing its diapers and putting the wet one away, the mother held the baby up in her arms.

"Thank you very much . . . Taki, come over here."

"It's all right. You can sit here." But the boy, without a word, stood up. As soon as he'd sat down across from me, he leaned against the window and began looking out.

"Oh, how rude." As if sorry for me, the woman apologized.

After a while, I asked: "How far are you going?"

"Hokkaido. To a place called Abashiri. I'm told it's awfully far and out of the way."

"Which district is it in?"

"Kitami."

"That's as far as you can go. It'll take you five days at least."

"I was told that even if we go straight through it takes a week."

The train was now pulling out of Mamada. From the nearby woods, the voice of the clear-toned cicadas seemed to accompany us. The sun had set. Passengers sitting on the west-facing side raised the sunshades. A cool breeze came in. The downy, inch-long hair of the baby, who had fallen asleep a short while ago in his mother's arms, trembled in the breeze. Near the baby's slightly open mouth, two or three flies flew around annoyingly. His mother, thinking about something, now and then chased them away with the handkerchief. After a while, clearing her things away, she laid the baby down. Taking two or three postcards and a pencil from the bag, she began to write. But she didn't get too far along.

"Mother." The boy, who had tired even of the scenery, spoke with sleepy eyes.

"What is it now?"

"Is it still far?"

"Yes, it's still a long ways. If you're sleepy, lean up against Mother and go to sleep."

"I'm not sleepy."

"Well, then, look at a picture book."

The boy silently nodded. From the cloth bundle, the mother took out four or five books and magazines. Docilely, the child began to look at them one by one. It was then, leaning back and watching the pair, that I realized that the boy's eyes, as he looked down at his picture book, and the mother's eyes, also lowered as she wrote her postcards, were exactly alike.

It surprises me—in a streetcar, say, as I look at a child sitting across from me with its parents—that either in the little face or figure the outward personalities of this man and woman who don't in the least resemble each other have been gracefully harmonized and made one. At first, looking at the child and its mother, I think they are very much alike. Then, looking at the child and its father, I think they too are very much alike. Lastly, looking at the mother and the father, I think it somehow strange that they don't resemble each other at all.

Remembering this kind of thing made me picture to myself the father from the child of this mother. It made me imagine what his present life was like.

Through a curious association of ideas, I easily summoned up the face and appearance of this woman's husband. At the Peers' School there had been a young court noble, Magaki, who wasn't that far ahead of me although he was five or six years older than I. I was reminded of that man. He was a big drinker. When he drank big, he talked big. A big man physically, with a pallid face and aquiline nose, he never studied. Having flunked his exams two or three times, he'd left school of his own accord. Sometime after the Russo-Japanese war, I had seen his name in the newspaper as the president of a company called the Joshu Hemp Joint Stock Corporation. I hadn't heard anything about him since then.

Suddenly recalling Magaki, I wondered if this woman's husband was not such a man. But Magaki had simply been a braggart. He wasn't that hard to get along with. There was even something genial and clownish about him. Of course, that kind of temperament is often undependable. Even the most genial man, after a series of failures, becomes difficult to live with. He turns moody. He becomes the sort of man who, to relieve his gloom somewhat, takes it out on a weak wife in a run-down household.

Might not the father of this child be such a person?

The woman was wearing a summer kimono, which, although old, was of crepe silk, and a grayish-blue obi. From them, I was able to imagine the winsome figure of this woman before and at the time of her marriage. I was also able to imagine her hardships since then.

The train, passing Oyama, passing Koganei, passing Ishibashi, sped on its way. Outside the window, the landscape had slowly darkened.

When the woman had finished two postcards, the boy said:

"Mother. I have to go." On this car, there was no toilet.

"Can't you wait a little longer?" the mother asked, at a loss. The boy, knitting his brows, nodded.

Putting her arms around the boy, the mother looked around, but couldn't think what to do.

"Just a little longer, h'm?" she earnestly comforted him. But the boy, shaking, said he might let go any minute.

Before long, the train arrived at Sunomiya. The mother spoke with the conductor, but was told there wasn't time here and to please wait until the next station. That was Utsunomiya, where there was a stop of eight minutes.

Until Utsunomiya, the mother must have been at her wit's end. The baby, who'd been asleep until now, opened its eyes. Giving it the breast, the mother kept repeating:

"Just a little longer, now, just a little longer." It occurred to me that if this woman wasn't led to her grave by her husband she would surely be finished off at some point by this child.

Roaring hollowly, the train slid into the station alongside the platform. Before it had stopped, the boy, hunched over and clutching his abdomen, was moaning: "Quick! Quick!"

"We'll go, now." The mother, placing the baby on the seat, put her face close up to it. "Be a good baby, and wait patiently." Saying this, she turned to me. "I'm sorry to give you so much trouble, but could you keep an eye on it?"

"Yes, of course," I answered gladly.

The train came to a stop. I quickly opened the door. The boy jumped down onto the platform.

"Be good, now." But the baby, as she was about to leave it, from behind the mother, reaching toward her, let out a scream as if it had been set on fire.

"Oh, dear." The mother hesitated a moment, then took out a long, slender child's obi of Hakata silk from the kerchief bundle. Passing it under the baby's arms, just before lifting the baby onto her back she took a cotton handkerchief from her sleeve and placed it on her nape. Deftly tying the obi, she shouldered the baby and stepped down onto the platform. Stepping down behind her, I said:

"Here's where I get off."

"Oh . . . is that so?" Although seemingly surprised, the woman formally bowed her head.

"Thank you so much for all your help."

Side by side, we began walking through the crowd on the platform.

"I'm sorry to ask you, but could you mail these postcards?" Saying this, she tried to take them out of the front of her kimono. But the crossed obi between her breasts kept her from getting at them. She came to a stop.

"Mother. What's the matter?" Turning around, the boy spoke as if scolding her.

"Wait a moment." Tucking in her chin, the mother tried to loosen the front of her kimono. The lobes of her ears grew red with the strain. Just then, I saw that the handkerchief, crumpled with the motions of carrying, had ridden up on one shoulder. Without a word, I put my hand to her shoulder to straighten it. Startled, the woman raised her eyes.

"The handkerchief's all wrinkled, so I . . ." I felt myself blush.

"I'm so sorry. Please." As I smoothed out the handkerchief, she stood perfectly still.

When, again without a word, I drew my hand away from her shoulder, the woman said once more: "I'm so sorry."

There, on the platform, without asking each other's name, we parted.

Postcards in hand, I came to the station entrance. There was a mailbox on the wall. I felt I would like to read the postcards. I also felt there would be no harm in doing so.

I hesitated a moment, but when I got to the mailbox I dropped each card into it address side up. As soon as I had, I wanted to take them out again. I'd glanced at the addresses as they went in. Both were addresses in Tokyo. One had a woman's name, the other a man's.

✲

✲

The Razor

✲

Yoshisaburo, of the Tatsudoko in Azabu-Roppongi, a man almost never ill, took to his bed with a very bad cold. The Festival of the Autumn Equinox being close at hand, it was a very busy time for his barber shop. As he lay in bed, Yoshisaburo regretted having fired his two shop boys, Genko and Jidako, the month before.

In the past, although a year or two older, Yoshisaburo had been a shop boy along with them. The previous master, taken with his skill with a razor, had given him his only daughter in marriage and retired shortly after, handing the shop over to him.

Genko, who had secretly desired the girl, quit immediately. But the good-natured Jidako, changing his manner of address from "Yoshi-san" to "Boss," worked hard and well as before. The old master died about six months later, followed by his wife in another six months or so.

In anything to do with the use of a razor, Yoshisaburo was truly a master. A man with a strong temper, moreover: if he stroked the skin and it was the least bit rough, he was not satisfied until pinching up the stubble hairs one by one he'd shaved it absolutely smooth. In doing this he never chafed the skin. Customers claimed that when they'd been shaven by Yoshisaburo, their one-day growth was not the same. He was proud of the fact that in ten years he had never so much as inadvertently nicked a customer's face.

About two years after he'd left, Genko straggled back, asking for his old job. Yoshisaburo, out of friendship for a former workmate, had rehired the apologetic Genko. But during those two years, Genko had gone to the bad. He was prone to neglect his work. Inveigling Jidako to go with him, he messed around with a dubious woman in Kasumicho who seemed to know a whole slew of soldiers. In the end, egging on the foolish Jidako, he even got him to pilfer money from the shop. Feeling sorry for Jidako, Yoshisaburo had often admonished him. But when it came to theft, there was nothing more he could do. About a month ago, he had fired both of them.

Now, there was an extremely pale, lethargic man of twenty called Kanejiro, and Kinko, a boy of twelve or thirteen whose head was abnormally long from front to back. At busy times before holidays, these two were good for nothing at all. Lying fever-racked in bed, Yoshisaburo felt a solitary annoyance.

As it neared noon, customers came crowding in. The noisy clatter of the glass door as it slid open and shut, the dry sound of Kinko's high, loose-toothed clogs as he shuffled about grated on Yoshisaburo's irritated nerves.

The glass door slid open again.

"It's from Yamada of the Ryudo. The master is leaving on a trip tomorrow night, so please sharpen this razor. I'll come back for it this evening." It was a woman's voice.

"We're sort of busy today. Wouldn't tomorrow morning be all right?" Kanejiro's voice asked.

The woman seemed to hesitate a minute.

"Well, by then without fail, then." Saying this, she slid the glass door shut, then reopening it right away added:

"Sorry to trouble you, but could you ask the boss to do it?"

"I don't know. The boss . . ." Kanejiro began. Interrupting him, Yoshisaburo shouted from his bed:

"Kané! I'll do it." His voice was sharp but husky. Not answering him, Kanejiro replied to the woman: "Very well." Closing the door, the woman seemed to go away.

"Damn." Muttering to himself, Yoshisaburo took out his arm, pallid and faintly stained from the blue-dyed underside of the quilt, and stared at it. But his body, weary from the fever, was as heavy as a firmly planted object. With drowsy eyes, he gazed at the sooty papier-mâché dog on the ceiling. Flies were clustered on the dog.

Without listening, he overheard the talk in the shop. Two or three soldiers, talking about such things as the quality of the small neighborhood restaurants and the foul taste of army chow, agreed that nonetheless when it got cool like this even that wasn't so bad. As he heard such talk, Yoshisaburo started to feel a little better. After a while, he languidly turned over on his side.

In the whitish, cloudy light of evening that came in at the kitchen door beyond the three-mat room, his wife O-Umé, the baby on her back, was getting supper ready. Savoring his lightened mood, he watched her.

"I'll do it now." Thinking this, he raised his heavy body on the bedding. But a dizzy spell forced him face down on his pillow for a while.

"Do you have to go?" Gently asking this, O-Umé, her wet hands dangling in front of her, came into the room.

Yoshisaburo meant to say no, but his voice didn't carry at all.

Pulling back the covers, O-Umé put the medicine bottles and the spit-pot to one side. Yoshisaburo tried again.

"It's not that," he managed to say. But his voice was so hoarse that O-Umé did not hear the words. His mood, which had begun to improve so slowly, turned sour again.

"Shall I hold you up from behind?" As if pitying him, O-Umé went around behind her husband.

"Bring me the leather strop and Yamada-san's razor." Yoshisaburo flung the words at her. O-Umé was silent a moment.

"Can you do it?"

"It's all right. Bring them."

". . . If you get up, you'll have to put on the sleeved coverlet."

"I told you it's all right and to bring them. Are you going to bring them now or not?" His voice was fairly low, but loaded with ill-humor. Pretending not to hear him, O-Umé got out the sleeved coverlet and put it on him from behind as he sat up tailor-style on the bedding. Lifting one hand onto his shoulder, Yoshisaburo grabbed the coverlet at the neck and tore it off himself.

Silently, O-Umé slid open the door of the half room and, stepping down into the dirt-floored entryway, brought back the strop and the razor. There being no place to hang the strop, she drove a bent nail into the housepost at Yoshisaburo's pillow.

Even at ordinary times, when he was in a bad mood Yoshisaburo was unable to strop a razor well. Now that his hands were shaking with fever, he could not at all sharpen it as he wished. O-Umé, who could not bear to watch him work himself into a rage, repeatedly said: "Why don't you let Kané do it?" But there was no answer. At last, though, Yoshisaburo's endurance gave out. After about fifteen minutes, as if both his will and strength were spent, he sank down on the bed again. Immediately sleepy, he dozed off.

At lamp-lighting time, Yamada's maid, saying she'd thought she'd try them again on the way back from her errands, took the razor with her.

O-Umé made up some rice gruel. She wanted to give it to Yoshisaburo before it got cold, but afraid that if she roused him from his exhausted sleep she would put him in a bad mood again, she held back. It got on toward eight o'clock. If she delayed too long, it would be past the time for his medicine. Forcing herself, she shook him awake. Yoshisaburo, not all that displeased, sat up and took some nourishment. Then, lying down, he fell asleep again at once.

A little before ten, Yoshisaburo was roused again for his medicine. This time, he lay drowsily awake, thinking of nothing in particular. His fever-hot breath, trapped by the edge of the quilt which he'd drawn up to his eyes, unpleasantly mantled his face. In the shop, too, it was dead quiet. Listlessly, he looked around him. On the housepost, the jet-black leather strop hung peacefully. The dim light of the lamp was tinged a disagreeable muddy reddish-yellow. In a corner, O-Umé, suckling the baby in bed, lay with her back bathed in the light. He felt as if the room itself were pulsating with fever.

"Boss . . . boss . . ." It was Kinko's timid voice, at the threshold from the entryway.

"Yes?" Yoshisaburo answered with his mouth muffled by the edge of the quilt. Whether his husky, suffocated-sounding voice was inaudible or not, Kinko again called: "Boss . . ."

"What is it?" This time his voice was sharp and clear.

"A razor has come again from Yamada-san."

"Another one?"

"No, the same one. He tried using it straightaway, but it didn't shave too well. He says it's all right if it's ready by tomorrow afternoon. He wants you to test it before sending it back."

"Is the maid there?"

"No, she's gone."

"Give it to me." Reaching his hand across the quilt, Yoshisaburo took the razor in its sheath from the respectfully prostrate Kinko.

"Your hands are unsteady with fever. Wouldn't it be better to give it to Yoshikawa-san in Kasumicho?"

Saying this, O-Umé drew her kimono together over her naked breasts and got up. Yoshisaburo, silently reaching out his hand, raised the wick of the lamp and taking the razor out of its sheath turned the blade over and over. Sitting by his pillow, O-Umé softly put her hand to his brow. With his free hand, Yoshisaburo brushed hers away as if it were a fly.

"Kinko!"

"Yes." Right at the edge of the bedding, Kinko answered.

"Bring the whetstone here."

"Yes."

When the whetstone was ready, Yoshisaburo sat up and with one knee folded began to hone the razor. Ten o'clock slowly chimed.

O-Umé, thinking it would do no good to say anything, sat by quietly.

After a while, having honed the razor, Yoshisaburo laid it against the leather strop. He felt as if the stagnant atmosphere of the room had begun to stir a little with the solid, stroking sound. Controlling his trembling hands, Yoshisaburo rhythmically stropped the blade, but do what he might it did not go well at all. Before long, the bent nail that O-Umé had put in as a makeshift hook abruptly popped out. Springing back at him, the strop wrapped itself around the razor.

"Ah! Dangerous!" Crying out, O-Umé looked fearfully at Yoshisaburo's face. His eyebrows were quivering.

Unwinding the strop, Yoshisaburo threw it down on the floor. Razor in hand, he got to his feet and, in nothing but his night-clothes, started for the entryway.

"You shouldn't do that . . ."

Lifting a tearful voice, O-Umé held him back. But he did not listen. Without a word, he went down into the entryway. O-Umé followed after him.

There were no customers in the shop. Kinko was sitting vacantly in the chair in front of the mirror.

"Where's Kané-san?" O-Umé asked.

"He's out dangling after Tokiko," Kinko answered with a serious face.

"What? He went out saying that's what he was after?" O-Umé burst into laughter. But Yoshisaburo had the same grim, set face as before.

Tokiko was a strange young woman whose family, five or six doors down, had a sign in front that said *Military Supplies and Sundries*. She was said to be a graduate of a girls' school. At that shop, there were always one or two soldiers, students, or neighborhood youths lounging around.

"We're closing, so you can go," O-Umé told Kinko.

"It's still early." Without reason, Yoshisaburo opposed her. O-Umé was silent.

Yoshisaburo started in honing the razor. Once he was properly seated, it went much better.

Bringing a cotton-padded jacket, O-Umé, with soothing words as if to a child, coaxed Yoshisaburo to put his arms through. Then, as if at last feeling easy, she sat on the threshold and watched Yoshisaburo's face as he honed away with all his might. Kinko, in the customer's chair by the window, hugging his knees, was shaving his hairless shins up and then down.

At this juncture, briskly opening the glass door, a short young man of twenty-two or -three entered. He was wearing a new *futako*-lined kimono with a waistband and low clogs whose thongs were as tight as they could be.

"I just need a once-over. I'm in a big hurry. Can you do me?" Saying this, he stopped abruptly in front of the mirror. Chewing his lower lip, he thrust out his jaw and rubbed it energetically with his fingertips. The young man's speech was that of the streets, but his accent was that of a youth from the country. From his knobbly fingers and his rugged, swarthy face, it was clear that during the day he worked at hard labor.

"Go get Kané-san. Quick." Motioning with her eyes, O-Umé ordered Kinko.

"I'll do it."

"Your hand isn't steady today. So . . ."

"I'll do it, I said." Yoshisaburo sharply cut her off.

"You're not yourself." O-Umé spoke in a low voice.

"My work-coat!"

"It's just a shave, after all. There won't be any hairs. Why not do it as you are?" O-Umé did not want him to take off the padded jacket.

Looking from the one to the other with a wondering face, the young man said:

"Is the boss sick?" As if flirting, he blinked his small, caved-in eyes.

"Yes, he has a slight cold . . ."

"They say there're some bad colds going around. You have to watch out."

"Thanks." Yoshisaburo spoke with bare courtesy.

When Yoshisaburo had tucked a white cloth around his neck, the young man said again: "I just need a once-over." Then, adding: "I'm in a hurry, you know what I mean?" he gave a little smirk. Silently against the thick of his arm, back and forth, Yoshisaburo stroked the blade of the just-now-sharpened razor.

"I like to be there by ten- or eleven-thirty," the youth went on. He wanted Yoshisaburo to say something.

Immediately, there floated up to Yoshisaburo's eyes a dirty woman in some dinky brothel, with a voice you could hardly tell was a woman's or a man's. When he thought that this vulgar little man would be making tracks from here to such a place, scenes that made him want to vomit passed one after another through his weakened mind. Dipping the soap into the completely tepid hot water, he savagely slapped on the lather from the jaw up to the cheeks. Even now, the youth continued to throw himself coquettish glances in the mirror. Yoshisaburo felt like pouring a stream of abuse over him.

Stropping the razor once more—*kyun, kyun*—Yoshisaburo started to shave from the throat upward, but the blade just would not cut as he wanted it to. And his hand was trembling. What's more, when he'd been lying down it hadn't been that bad, but now that he was standing with his face downward, watery mucus at once began to drip from his nose. From time to time, he stopped shaving and wiped it with the back of his hand, but soon afterward the tip of his nose again began to itch and the mucus gathered into a drop all ready to fall.

From inside, there was the sound of the baby crying. O-Umé went back in to it.

Even while being shaved with a blade that didn't cut well, the young man had a placid look on his face. It didn't seem to hurt or tickle him. Such stolid lack of concern got on Yoshisaburo's nerves until he was in a fury. Although one of his own blades would have cut smoothly, he did not change to it. His feeling was that nothing mattered anymore. Even so, at some point he'd turned meticulous again. If a place was the least bit rough, he had to go over it. The more he went over it, the angrier he became. His body slowly grew weary. His mind, too, was weary. The fever seemed to have grown worse.

The young man, who at first had talked of this and that, afraid now of Yoshisaburo's bad humor, fell silent. By the time the razor was at his temples, he'd begun to doze off from the fatigue of his hard work during the day. Kinko, too, leaning back against the window, was catnapping. Even the voice of O-Umé, crooning to the baby, had stopped. It was dead quiet. The night, inside and outside the house, was as still as the grave. There was only the scraping sound of the razor.

His fretful, angry mood turned into a feeling of wanting to cry. His body and mind were utterly exhausted. He felt as if his eyes were melting from inside with the fever.

When he had shaved from the throat to the cheeks, the jaw, and the temples, there was one soft part of the throat that just would not go right. After all the trouble he'd taken, he felt like slashing it off, skin and all. As he looked at that face, with its coarse-grained skin, the oil collecting in each of the pores, he felt that way from his heart. The young man had fallen asleep. His head dropped way back, his mouth gaped open. His irregular, yellow teeth were revealed.

The exhausted Yoshisaburo could neither stand nor sit. He felt as if poison had been poured into each and every one of his joints. He wanted to throw it all away, to drop down on the ground and roll around. Enough! he thought to himself any number of times. But by force of habit, he kept at it.

. . . Just slightly, the blade caught. The young man's throat twitched jerkily. From the top of his head to the tip of his toes, something passed swiftly through Yoshisaburo. It took with it all his weariness and disgust.

The cut was quite small. He stood there, simply looking at it. At first, between the thin little flaps of skin, a milky white color; then a faint crimson, steadily dyeing the cut. Abruptly, blood welled up. He stared at it. The blood darkened and swelled into a globule. Reaching its maximum distension, the drop flattened and streaked down the throat. A sort of rough, raging emotion surged up in Yoshisaburo.

Yoshisaburo had never cut the face of a customer in his life. The emotion came upon him with extraordinary force. His breath grew shallow and fast. It was as if he were being pulled body and soul into the cut. There was nothing he could do, now, to resist that feeling. Shifting the blade point downward, he plunged it deep into the throat. The blade was completely hidden. The young man did not even stir.

A moment later, the blood gushed out. Quickly, the young man's face turned the color of clay.

Almost in a faint, Yoshisaburo, as if falling, sat down in a chair alongside. His tension immediately went out of him, and his extreme fatigue came back. Dead tired, closing his eyes, he looked like a corpse. The night, too, was as still as a corpse. All movement was in abeyance. Everything was sunk in a deep sleep. Only the mirror, from three sides, coldly regarded this scene.

✲

✲

The Paper Door

✲

My friend and I, as the sun went down, arrived at a certain hot spring in the mountains. Although we hadn't been hiking, the buttock-cramping fatigue of being bounced along the mountain roads in a rickshaw left us ready for bed. Laying white cushions on our chests, we smoked cigarettes and talked.

"Whenever I come to a hot spring, there's a story I remember. Perhaps I've already told it to you," my friend said.

"What kind of story?"

"It took place at the Kinokuniya in Ashi no yu. Back when the present Kikugoro called himself Ushinosuké. Almost ten years ago."

"I haven't heard any story with Ushinosuké in it."

"He's not in it himself, but a girl who looked like him is."

"I haven't heard it." I shook my head.

"I'll tell it, then. It's about when I was loved." My friend began:

On the third floor of the Kinokuniya, there was a large room that had been divided. Since it was summer, the hotel was full. Both my grandparents, myself, my youngest sister, who was then in kindergarten, and her maid were all put up in half of that room. In the other half, separated from us by a single paper door, there was another party of five. It comprised a couple—the husband was said to be a lawyer in Kyobashi—the mother (a lady of about fifty who looked strong-minded and young for her age), a little girl of four or so, who was not just pretty but as beautiful as a doll, called Minori, and her maid.

The wife was willowy and tall, with an extremely stylish figure. By her way of speaking, she seemed to be the daughter of a rich family. In the evening, she often sang excerpts from *naga uta,** accompanying herself on a samisen. Sometimes, on that samisen, she would chant ballad-dramas of the old days in a low voice. Every morning, she would teach the child Minori a song.

The two children would soon have become friends in any event. The morning after our arrival, though, when the song practice next door began, my sister immediately went out onto the veranda. Leaning back on her hands against the railing, rubbing her back against it, she quietly edged forward and peeped into the next room.

When the stanza was over, the lady called out: "Please come in." My sister, digging her chin into her chest and looking very solemn in a way children have, said nothing. I winked at our maid, Hana. Hana went out, and from then on my sister and Minori were friends.

We'd already been there ten days or so. Minori possessed a great many folk toys from Hakoné. When the mists had cleared off, she would take them out onto the large sun deck on the roof of the second floor and play there with my sister. Suzu, the maid next door, and our Hana were of an age. Leaving the children on their own, the two became close friends.

This Suzu looked very much like Ushinosuke.

Not long before, at the Tokyo Theater, I'd seen a farce featuring Chobei of the Kakitsu (not the Hanzuin), Kanbei of the Karasu-yama, and somebody Sarunosuké as the villains. Suzu looked just like the country maiden, I forget her name, played by Ushinosuké. It had been my first glimpse of the theater. Those days, when there was a farce performed by the Kabuki, I wasn't content until I had seen each play twice over. The actors

*An epic folk ballad. (translator's note)

had only recently graduated from child roles. Ushinosuké, whose voice was changing, was as beautiful as a girl. I liked him the best.

From that association, I quickly came to like Suzu too. Of course, it was merely a slight attraction . . .

Her naive dark face, as plump as if it would burst, and her sparkling eyes went straight to my heart. A country girl, she didn't say much. You could tell at a glance that she was a good person, who didn't know the world. Hana, a Tokyoite, easily had the best of her when they talked together.

When I went with my sister for a walk or to the playground for a ride on the swing, Suzu, even if Hana wasn't around, would coax Minori along and follow us. It was that open. Even when, as Minori's playmate, she was doing something else, as soon as I got ready to go out she would put all the toys away and come after me. She must have been fifteen or so; I believe I was about eighteen. We didn't have much to say to each other, even when we walked together like this. More and more, though, I had a lonely feeling when Suzu didn't come along. Even if I had an errand to do, I would wait a while for her.

Back then there weren't any picture postcards of actors. Buying directly from the Moriyama shop in Shintomi-cho, just about the only place that had them, I collected actors' photographs. A friend of mine, Hayashi, who'd introduced me to the theater, had had one of the late Kikugoro as the young priest Benten reduced at the Kogawa shop in Hiyoshi-cho and wore it on his watch chain in a frame as small as the ball of his thumb. I, too, had Hayashi get me one of Ushinosuké, and wore it on my chain. I'd brought many other photographs of Ushinosuké with me. But I thought it very inconvenient that I couldn't gaze at them to my heart's content in front of my grandparents. It's strange what I did instead, but anyway, I started looking at Suzu's face now and again. At some point, it became a habit.

In everyday life, one does not ordinarily stare at a person's face as when one studies a face in a photograph or a person on the stage. Even for those who are constantly exposed to the public, being looked at is something they feel particularly. All the more did Suzu, no matter how carefree, have to take notice when I looked at her so often and so hard.

When I say this, it sounds indecent, as if I thought only I were a good boy. But the truth is that I liked Suzu because she resembled Ushinosuké. Because her face reminded me of Ushinosuké's, I wanted to go on walks with her.

It wasn't long before something peculiar began to happen. As I gazed intently into Suzu's face, she now and then looked back at me in the same way.

As I sat reading at a little table of lacquered papier mâché loaned me by the inn, which I had placed near the veranda, I would suddenly get the feeling that Suzu was not far off, watching me. And in fact this was so. I could not understand why she was looking at me so hard. No doubt she was very fond of me, but to glue her eyes on my face because of that seemed somewhat odd. Afterwards, I had this thought: might it not be that Suzu, taking my rude scrutiny as a sign that I was in love with her, began to gaze earnestly into my face to show that she, too, was in love with me? It may have been something like that. An innocent country girl might well have thought that way. But when it came to that, even though I liked Suzu, I felt rather uncomfortable. I was unable to look at her face as before.

Perhaps at this point I should say something more about the family next door. The wife was a very good person. I liked her very much. Her husband was a disagreeable person, and I disliked him. A pallid, effeminate fellow, he wore a bushy reddish moustache. The mother, a sharp-nosed lady as lean as a rail, wore her abundant black hair cut and let down, with a flat chignon. An extremely quick-tempered person, she always had to have her own way. One night, this kind of thing happened: At eight-thirty or so, the lady had summoned a masseuse and was having a medical rubdown. My grandfather, calling the maid, said to her: "Please ask the masseuse to come here when she's through next door." This must have been heard next door, and we could hear the maid telling the masseuse. It was not likely the lady didn't know about it. Towards ten, when her massage was nearly over at last, the lawyer came back from a game of *go* or the like. "When I lose, my shoulders feel stiffer than usual," he remarked, allowing as how he might have a massage himself. The wife, having gone to the bath or privy, was not in the room. Positive that the lady, who knew we were waiting, would speak to him, we listened intently. But she said nothing. The man had himself massaged for upwards of an hour. After he was all finished, the lady's words were: "My own massage has been cut horribly short."

By the time the masseuse came to us, my grandfather was in bed and sound asleep. I sent her away. The mother, who was like this at all times, also found fault with everything in a shrill, carrying voice. When the menu was brought, she and she alone must choose the dishes. And so, although the children were the best of friends, the adults had almost nothing to do with each other.

One night, I read in bed until about midnight. Then I turned off the light to go to sleep. Although ours was a ten-mat room, with three sets of bedding laid out it was pretty close quarters. So as to leave a space on the far side where one could get by, I lay right alongside the sliding paper door that partitioned the two rooms. Next to mine was my grandfather's bedding, and next to his my grandmother's. My sister, putting down a quilt that overlapped the edges of theirs, slept in between them. By comparison, Hana, at my grandmother's feet, had plenty of room.

Suddenly, at a sound, I opened my eyes. The paper door, which reached across the room in four panels, was softly sliding open. Wonderingly, I raised my head from the pillow. The panel, about two-thirds of the way open, softly, quietly slid shut again. As it was farther down the room than I was, and with only the dim light of a paper lantern in either room, I could not make out who had done such a thing, nor why. But right away I thought of Suzu. How bold of her, I thought. And why had she done it? Thinking that perhaps Suzu really had begun to fall in love with me, I felt something a little bit like happiness. Not really caring, though, I soon fell asleep again.

The next morning, until I was in the bath and happened to remember, I'd forgotten all about it. Even when I did remember, it somehow seemed like a dream.

At breakfast, it was mealtime in the next room as well.

"Last night, that panel over there opened," we heard the mother say.

"Yes, it opened all right," the lawyer said, with a small laugh.

We heard this quite distinctly. But both my grandfather and grandmother were silent.

"Suzu. Did you notice anything?" asked the mother, her voice rising slightly. For a moment, Suzu seemed stuck for a reply. Then she said:

"No. Nothing."

"You mean you don't know about it? But the panel's right by where you were sleeping." The mother's tone was scornful.

"It doesn't matter, does it?" As if reproaching the mother, the wife put strength into her low voice.

At this point, I could not stay silent any longer.

"Madam. I know about the door opening too," I called out in a deliberate, loud voice. "Keep quiet," my grandfather said to me with his eyes, trying to restrain me.

"The young man next door says he knows about it. Who opened it, then?" the mother demanded agitatedly. "The young man next door" had an unpleasant sound to it. I began to get angry, but my grandfather gave me a stern look. I forced myself to be silent.

"Didn't you open it, Suzu?" the indomitable mother continued.

"No. I don't like this." Suzu's slow country speech was like a bucket of water thrown over the conversation. Although she hadn't said anything to lay the blame on me, once Suzu had doused all further talk it was just as if I *had* been blamed. It made me sulky.

"Mother, haven't you said enough?" The wife seemed to be thinking what a shame it all was. It sounded to me as if they had been through this sort of thing many times.

"Of course, it's possible that everyone was too sleepy to know what was going on," said the lawyer, who until then had fallen silent.

"You speak of it so lightly. This time it was just a door being open, so no harm has been done, but Suzu is about to be a bride. I don't know if any of you are aware of it, but the night before last the door was also opened about a foot. Did you know that?"

"I knew," answered the lawyer. It sounded as if he were smiling.

This startled me. I am a very light sleeper, and felt sure that I would have awakened immediately at anything out of the ordinary. But of this I knew nothing.

"In this heat, we cannot go back to the city. And there are people in the next room, so we've got to put up with this paper door. But I will not stand for this constant opening of it."

"Grandfather, it was not I who opened that door," I appealed to him exasperatedly.

My grandfather, smiling slightly, gave me a light nod.

"When you've had your breakfast, we'll go for a walk."

Intensely annoyed, I left the room right away. After a while my grandfather, in a pair of slippers and a big gray hat like a helmet, a walking stick on his shoulder, came downstairs to the entryway where I was waiting.

"Shall we walk towards Benten Mountain?" he asked. I replied:

"The view from there is probably the best." Back then the new road hadn't been put through yet. Walking along the mountain road that was more like a dry streambed, we talked.

My grandfather told me a story about the Zen priest Hakuin.

It is a famous story, and I've heard it since from many different people. It seems that a certain maiden, becoming pregnant, was asked by her father who the baby's father was. In desperation, the girl said it was the high priest Hakuin. I forget the other circumstances, but anyway, her father was overjoyed and rushed off to the temple. When he told the priest, Hakuin is reported merely to have said: "Ah, so?" In due course of time, the real father's identity became known. Absolutely flabbergasted, the girl's father went back to make an abject apology. When he was done, Hakuin again said merely: "Ah, so?"

It was a pertinent story, and it took me right out of my bad mood. When we got back, the family next door was busy packing its things. After they'd had lunch, three rickshaws arrived. Only the wife, looking as if she were sorry things had turned out this way, came by briefly to say good-bye. She said they were going down to the Tsutaya in Sokokura.

As for Suzu, she of the carefree face that resembled Ushinosuke's, she was just about heartbroken. The spirit had gone out of her. Suddenly feeling sorry for her, I wanted to say something, but didn't say anything. Only Hana saw them off as far as the entryway. The lawyer, in a Western suit, walked about supervising the rickshawmen. I watched them until they were out of sight around Benten Mountain.

That was the last I saw of Suzu. In ten years, we haven't met even once. But the year after that, at a charity performance of the Kabuki, I saw the lawyer, his wife, and Minori in one of the boxes. Their new maid, a girl of fifteen or sixteen, had a more intelligent face than Suzu's. In the corridor leading to the restrooms, the wife and I passed each other, but pretended not to recognize one another.

That is the story. But if I may say a last word on behalf of Suzu who loved me, when she opened the door that time, it wasn't with any lewd intention (open the door, and then what). No, we're talking about a dumb country girl. When she did that, she must have been thinking that to stare into another person's face was a way to reveal one's love. She must have been trying to show her love for me.

So my friend, neatly and easily tacking on the conclusion (perhaps because he had done so so many times), completed this story about when he was loved.

✲

✲

Seibei and His Gourds

✲

This is the story of a boy called Seibei and his gourds. Later Seibei gave up his gourds, but he soon found something to take their place. It was drawing pictures, and he was now as enthusiastically absorbed by that as he'd once been by gourds . . .

Both his parents knew that Seibei now and then came home with some gourd he'd bought. He must have brought as many as ten, with the skins on, ranging in price from three or four sen to as high as fifteen sen. By himself, he skillfully cut them open and removed the seeds. He made his own plugs. First taking away the bad smell with tea dregs, he assiduously polished the gourds with leftover saké of his father's which he had saved.

Certainly, Seibei's devotion was fanatical. One day, he was walking along the shore road, as usual thinking and thinking about gourds, when something caught his eye. It startled him. It was the bald head of an old man who had stepped out from a row of stalls that lined the road with their backs to the sea. Seibei thought it was a gourd. "What a magnificent gourd!" he thought. It was a while before he realized his error. When he did, he felt surprised at himself. The old man, wagging his finely colored head, entered an alley across the way. Suddenly amused, Seibei laughed out loud. Laughing like crazy, he ran for half a block. Even then, he couldn't stop laughing.

Such was his devotion that, when walking in town, he would always stop to gaze at any shop with gourds hung from the eaves, be it an antique shop, a kitchenware store, a candy store, or a shop that specialized in gourds.

Seibei, eleven years old, was still in grade school. Often when he'd come home, rather than playing with the other children, he would set out alone for town to look at gourds. At night, sitting tailor-style in a corner of the parlor, he would work on a gourd. When it was ready, he would pour in the sake dregs, wrap it in a towel, and after putting it in a can place it in the sunken hearth. Then he would go to bed. In the morning, as soon as he got up he would open the can. After gazing insatiably at the gourd, covered all over with sweat, he would carefully attach a thread, hang the gourd from a sunny part of the eaves, and go off to school.

In Seibei's town, there was a commercial district and a harbor so that it was fairly busy. But one could walk through the relatively small area of the long, narrow town in twenty minutes or so. Therefore, although there were many shops that sold gourds, Seibei, who'd spent nearly all his spare time walking around and looking, had probably seen all the gourds there were to see.

He didn't have much interest in old gourds. His taste was for those with their skins on, that had not yet been cut open. Furthermore, those he chose were for the most part of the so-called gourd shape (scorned by connoisseurs) and of a comparatively commonplace appearance.

"This kid of yours, when it comes to gourds, only picks the ugly ones." Watching as Seibei, off to the side, zealously polished a gourd, a guest who had come to visit his carpenter father made this comment.

"He's always messing with gourds or something else, even though he's just a kid," the father said ill-humoredly, looking around at him.

"Sei-boy. It won't do just to bring home that uninteresting kind of gourd. Why don't you buy something a little more original?" the guest asked.

"This one is fine," Seibei calmly answered.

The conversation of the guest and Seibei's father turned to the general subject of gourds.

"At the exhibition this spring, there was a splendid gourd that's said to have belonged to Bakin," Seibei's father said.

"Was it quite a large gourd?"

"It was big, and it was long."

Hearing this kind of talk, Seibei smiled within himself. "Bakin's gourd" was a celebrated object of the time. But just one look—Seibei didn't know who Bakin was, but quickly deciding the gourd was a thing of no value, he'd left the exhibition hall.

"I didn't care for that gourd. It was nothing but big," Seibei put in.

When he heard this, the father, round-eyed with anger, barked:

"What would you know about it? Shut up!"

Seibei was silent.

One day, walking along a back street, Seibei came to an unfamiliar place. In front of the lattice of a residential shop, an old woman had set up a stand of dried persimmons and tangerines. On the latticework, she'd hung out about twenty gourds. At once, saying: "Please, just let me take a look," Seibei stepped up and examined them one by one. Among them was one about five inches around, at first sight of such an ordinary shape that he wanted to hug it, it was so good.

Heart thudding, he inquired:

"How much is this one?" The old woman replied:

"For you, sonny, I'll knock it down to ten sen." Breathing hard, Seibei said:

"If that's so, don't sell it to anyone else. I'll come back right away with the money." After repeating this, he set off at a run for his house.

In no time at all, face flushed, gasping for breath, Seibei was back. Receiving the gourd, he went off again at a run.

From then on, he would not let the gourd out of his sight. He even started taking it to school. In the end, once, he even polished it under his desk during a class. The teacher detected him. It being the ethics class, he was all the more infuriated.

The teacher, who was from another part of the country, could not abide the fact that the people of this locality took an interest in such things as gourds. A devotee of the samurai ethic, he went to hear Kumoemon three of the days of his four-day engagement at a small theater in the brothel district, which ordinarily he was afraid even to pass through. Although he was not all that annoyed by the songs that the pupils made up about him on the playground, his voice shook with anger over Seibei's gourd. "You are a person with absolutely no prospects in life," he told him. The gourd to which Seibei had given such loving care and effort was taken away from him on the spot. Seibei could not even cry.

When, his face pale, he'd come home, he sat down in a daze on the edge of the sunken hearth.

Just then, the teacher, carrying his textbooks in a bundle, came to see Seibei's father. Out on a job, the father was not at home.

"I must ask you to deal with this kind of thing yourselves . . ." Saying this, the teacher lit into Seibei's mother. The mother merely cringed with shame.

Seibei was suddenly afraid of the teacher's implacability. His lips trembling, he made himself small in a corner of the room. On the housepost, right in back of the teacher, hung many finished gourds. Thinking "Will he notice them now, will he notice them now," Seibei was in a panic.

After he'd given the mother a stern talking to, the teacher, without having noticed the gourds, at last went away. Seibei breathed a sigh of relief. His mother, bursting into tears, commenced a long, grumbling scolding.

Before long, Seibei's father came back from the construction site. When he heard what had happened, he abruptly grabbed Seibei, who was sitting off to one side, and beat him. Here also, Seibei was told: "You have no future at all, you brat."

"A fool like you—get out," he was told.

Suddenly noticing the gourds on the housepost, Seibei's father took a big hammer and smashed them one by one. Seibei, simply turning pale, said nothing.

The teacher, as if the gourd he'd confiscated from Seibei was a dirty thing, as if throwing it away, gave it to the old man who was the school janitor. Taking it home, the janitor hung it up on the housepost of his small, soot-darkened room.

About two months later, the janitor, hard up for a little cash, had the idea of selling the gourd for whatever it would fetch. Taking it to the neighborhood curio dealer, he showed it to him.

The dealer looked at it with squinting scrutiny. Suddenly cold-faced, he shoved it back at the janitor.

"I'll take it off your hands for five yen."

The janitor was dumbfounded. But he was a shrewd fellow. His face expressionless, he answered:

"I can't possibly let it go for so little."

The dealer immediately raised his offer to ten yen. But the janitor still held out.

Finally, the dealer just barely managed to obtain the gourd for fifty yen. The janitor was secretly overjoyed at his good fortune, at having gotten from the teacher free something worth four months of his salary. To the end, though, he kept on his know-nothing face, not only with the teacher, but with Seibei. So that nobody knew where the gourd had gone.

But even the crafty janitor could not have imagined that the dealer had sold the gourd to a local rich collector for five hundred yen.

Seibei was now enthusiastically absorbed in his drawing. He no longer felt any resentment toward the teacher nor his father who had smashed more than ten of his cherished gourds with a hammer.

Before long, though, the father began to berate him for drawing pictures.

✲

✲

An Incident

✲

It was a sultry late-July afternoon. There was not a breath of air. Along the tracks that gleamed like twin streaks of mercury, the trolley raced ahead with a monotonous clickety-clack, clickety-clack. There was almost nobody about. The only persons in sight were an ice cream vendor, who had set up his stall in front of a high concrete wall, and a single customer squatting there and fanning himself. Above the two, a fig tree extended its slack-looking branches from inside the wall. Its leaves, starting to curl up in a sickly way, coated with thin dust, were completely and eerily still. As I leaned against the frame of the frontmost window, where at least there was a slight breeze, my mind was absolutely blank. A half-read magazine, its pages still turned back, was rolled up in my sweaty hand.

The trolley stopped. No one got on or off. As if bored, the trolley ran on to the next stop. Here a buxom woman of about forty got on. She held a small sateen umbrella in one hand, a soaked handcloth in the other, with which she continually mopped her throat. Her face was flushed and sweaty. Some of the passengers turned a drowsy eye on her, but most of them did not stir from their half-asleep postures of fatigue.

There were eight or nine passengers. In front of me sat a young man in a uniform and a beret with the badge of an electric company, dozing with an ill-humored expression. Next to him a couple of students, the brims of their straw hats drawn down over their faces and their legs asprawl, slumbered in grim poses. Their bare feet were blackly smeared with perspiration and grime that shaded off to a whitish dust on their shins. They gave off a feeling of oppressive heat and squalor. There was a big man of fifty or so, in a Western suit, who looked like some minor official. A dirty imitation panama shoved far back on his head, his chin resting on a cane propped between his knees, thinking of nothing at all, he wore a completely vacant expression. His eyes were open, but were not focused on anything. Still, he seemed to be aware of my looking at him. Leaning back, the man narrowed his eyes and resumed his empty revery. Then, abruptly, with a nappy cotton handkerchief crumpled up in his palm, he wiped his broad, balding forehead. In the intense sunlight, I too could not keep my eyes fully open. Even squinting, it hurt to look at anything. I began to resent this disagreeable heat, pressing down on me like an unjust corporal punishment. How stupid, I thought, to wear raingear for wet weather and warm clothing for cold weather, only to have to bear the full brunt of hot weather and be prostrated by it.

Suddenly, a white butterfly flew in at the window. Buoyantly, like a tiny rubber ball, it flitted here and there with a solitary liveliness, as if happily and insanely busy.

The trolley ran on with the same monotonous clickety-clack. Drugged by the heat, as if they'd even forgot where they were going and with what in mind, the passengers sat sunk in stupor. The butterfly, not knowing it had already been transported several hundred yards, fluttered about playfully. My heat-heavy brain, swathed in torpor, was diverted somewhat by the eye-bewildering zigzags of this little wag.

All of a sudden the butterfly bumped against the ceiling two, three times in a row. Failing to find a foothold, it alighted on a theater advertisement below. Its thickly powdered, pure white and powerfully bright wings and the jet-black woodblock characters, drawn in the broad strokes of the Kantei style of calligraphy, announcing a special Kabuki engagement, made a beautiful contrast. As if to catch its breath after its hectic frolics, the butterfly was abruptly and utterly still. The trolley simply ran on monotonously as before. The passengers sat slumped down in their seats in the same semi-lethargy. My mind, too, was empty again.

Several dull moments went by. Suddenly, at the peculiar yelling of the motorman, I raised my head. Up ahead, a little boy was about to cut across the tracks. Not once looking our way, he was running as hard as he could. But it was more of a light-hearted scamper. He hadn't yet run inside the tracks. Shouting, the motorman yanked back on the brake. The trolley had already slowed down a lot. All the same, it and the boy seemed headed for the intersection of their lines of direction to meet in a senseless, inevitable collision. Already it seemed too late to do anything. As the boy vanished underneath the railing of the motorman's platform, there was a sickening thud. The trolley slid forward another six feet or so. From a sudden instinctive sense that I could not stay put, I'd dodged far in back of the conductor. Holding down my trembling, I stared at everybody's backs. Then the boy's wailing voice arose. I felt relief. (This relief was more of a selfish feeling than anything else. But even afterwards, it gave me pleasure.)

Going up front, I wedged myself among the other passengers and peered out the window. A crowd was already gathering from the nearby houses. Cursing a blue streak, the young man from the electric company took up the violently wailing boy and glared about him. He seemed to have worked himself into a fury. The boy, his short summer kimono ridden up to his chest in the man's grasp, comely little buttocks exposed, legs doubled up, screamed at the top of his lungs. His homely, sweaty face and big head looked all the funnier for it.

"It's all right, it's all right," said the conductor soothingly, stroking the boy's buttocks.

"Take another look," the young man said, as if angrily. Turning the boy upside down, he hoisted up his buttocks. The big man who seemed to be a minor official had come over.

"We should take a close look," the man said, sounding worried. He peered at the boy.

"He's all right. Not even scratched," the conductor announced after a brief examination.

A short way off, lowering the lever of the cowcatcher, his face completely expressionless, the motorman said in a cold voice:

"A good thing the net caught him."

"Yes! It certainly was lucky!" exclaimed the bureaucrat, turning around.

"Hey!" shouted the young man holding the boy. "Where's his family?"

"They've just now gone to get them," one of the onlookers answered.

The boy, who until now had merely been wailing and screaming, arched back and started writhing to escape the young man's grip. As the young man got angry, he struggled harder. He began to pound the young man's face.

"You goddam brat!" With a fierce expression, the young man held him at arm's length and glared at him.

His old panama still pushed back on his head, hanging about somehow uneasily, the bureaucrat said in a low voice as if to himself:

"It was lucky. It certainly was lucky." Then, going up to the boy, he said:

"You can stop crying now." He stroked the boy's cheek, coated with a dirty makeup of tears, sweat, and dust. Although he'd been struggling so hard, the boy didn't try to hit the kindhearted bureaucrat. Squatting, the man examined the boy's buttocks and legs. Docile now, the boy held still.

"Here, this won't do!" the bureaucrat exclaimed. The attention of the onlookers, who had begun to disperse, was quickly focused again.

"The little guy's taken a piss," announced the bureaucrat. Everyone burst into laughter.

Silently, his eyes still angry, the young man looked down at himself. The lower part of his shirt was soaking wet. Everyone burst out laughing again. Squeezed between his bunched-up thighs, like a pretty little gourd, the tip of the boy's penis was still wet.

"Damn. I've had it with this brat." Bear-hugging the child, the young man rapped his chin against his head a couple of times. The boy commenced wailing again.

"Now, now. A little piss is nothing," the bureaucrat said placatingly. From among the onlookers, a voice called out: "Here she comes! Here she comes!" Beside herself with excitement, a dark-skinned, homely woman was running toward them. Grabbing the boy from the young man, she glared at him fiercely. Exclaiming "You fool!" she started slapping him around the head fast and hard. The boy wept and screamed even louder. Gripping him, the mother gave her writhing, kicking offspring a couple of good shakes. "Fool!" The young man, who had been looking on with a frown, interrupted the punishment.

"After all, madam, it's your fault." The two began to argue with each other.

A little way off, the bureaucrat was walking around and talking to himself in an agitated manner. The motorman was already on his way back to the driver's platform. The bureaucrat called out after him again:

"You. It certainly was lucky." Almost unmeaningly, he tapped his cane at the safety fender. Then, once again: "It certainly was lucky. This thing must never have worked so well." His words didn't seem to adequately contain his happy agitation. He seemed to want to say more. But he couldn't find the words to say it. The motorman gave him a rather cold look.

The crowd had already broken up. Most people had withdrawn under the eaves of the houses and were looking on from there.

The mother strenuously thanked the conductor. The boy,

mouth and nose submerged in her large, slackly pendulous breasts, was completely submissive now.

The young man and the bureaucrat got on the trolley again. Picking up the boy's clogs, the mother started home. The trolley got underway.

Briskly removing his uniform jacket, the young man stripped off his urine-soaked shirt. His white skin and compact physique appeared. Rolling up the shirt, he busily swabbed his stomach and abdomen. The muscles of his shoulders, arms, and chest worked pleasingly. He raised his eyes a moment, catching mine across the aisle. He smiled at me.

"This is too much." The ferocious countenance of before, as if his blood were up, was entirely gone. In its place was a pleasant, lively, good-natured look.

The buxom woman and the bureaucrat had started up a conversation. The bureaucrat gestured and spoke animatedly.

The two students had also begun to chat.

These people who before, succumbing to the heat, had been quasi-comatose, had now all come alive.

I too, now, experienced a pleasurable excitement.

When I thought to look, the innocent little sport of a butterfly, that had been perched on the theater advertisement, had flown away and was nowhere in sight.

✲

✲

Han's Crime

✲

In an unusual incident, a young Chinese juggler called Han severed his wife's carotid artery during a performance with a knife the size of a carver. The young wife died on the spot. Han was immediately arrested.

The act was witnessed by the owner-manager of the troupe, a Chinese stagehand, the introducer, and an audience of over three hundred. A policeman, sitting on a chair set up slightly above and at the edge of the audience, also saw it. But it was not at all known whether this incident, which had occurred before so many eyes, was a deliberate act or an accident.

For this performance, Han made his wife stand in front of a thick board the size of a rain shutter. From a distance of twelve feet, he hurled several of the carver-sized knives, each with a shout, to form an outline of her body not two inches removed from it.

The judge commenced by interrogating the owner-manager.

"Is that performance a particularly difficult one?"

"No. For an experienced performer, it is not that difficult. All that's required is an alert, healthy state of mind."

"If that's so, an incident like this should not have happened even as a mistake."

"Of course, unless one is sure of the performer—extremely sure—one cannot allow the performance."

"Well, then. Do you think it was a deliberate act?"

"No. I don't. The performance requires experience, instinctive skill and nothing else. But one cannot say that it will always come off with a machinelike precision. It's a fact that we never thought something like this would happen. But I do not think it is fair, now that it *has* happened, to say that we had considered the possibility and hold it against us."

"Well, what do you think it was?"

"I don't know."

The judge was perplexed. There was, here, the fact of homicide. But there was absolutely no proof as to whether it was premeditated murder or manslaughter (if the former, the judge thought, there was never such a cunning murder as this). Next calling in the Chinese stagehand, who had served with the troupe longer than Han, the judge questioned him.

"What is Han's ordinary behavior like?"

"He's a good person. He doesn't gamble, fool around with other women, or drink. About a year ago, he converted to Christianity. His English is good, and when he has the time he often reads collections of sermons."

"And his wife?"

"She was a good person too. As you know, people of our sort aren't always known for their strict morals. One often hears of somebody running off with somebody else's wife. Han's wife was a beautiful woman, although on the small side, and she now and then got solicitations of that sort. But she never took up with such people."

"What were their dispositions like?"

"Toward others, they were both extremely kind and gentle. They never thought of themselves and never got angry. And yet" (here the stagehand paused. Thinking a moment, he went on) "I'm afraid this may be to Han's detriment, but to tell the truth, strangely enough, those two, who were so kind, gentle, and self-effacing with others, when it came to their own relationship, were surprisingly cruel to each other."

"Why was that?"

"I don't know why."

"Had they always been that way?"

"No. About two years ago, the wife gave birth. The baby was premature, and died in three days or so. But after that, it was clear even to us that their relationship was slowly going to the bad. They would often have arguments over the most trivial things. At such times, Han would suddenly turn dead pale. But in the end, no matter what, he always fell silent. He never mistreated his wife. Of course, that's most likely because his religion forbade him to. But sometimes, when you looked at his face, there was a terrible, uncontrollable anger in it. Once, I suggested that if things were so bad between them it might be good to get a divorce. But Han said that even if his wife had reasons for seeking a divorce, he himself had none. Han followed his own will in the matter. He even said that there was no way he could love his wife. It was only natural, he said, if a woman he did not love gradually came not to love him. It was why he took to reading the Bible and collections of sermons. He seemed to think that by somehow calming his heart he could correct his fairly unruly feelings of hatred. After all, he had no reason to hate his wife. She, too, deserved sympathy. After their marriage, they had travelled about as road-players for nearly three years. Owing to an older brother's profligacy, the family back home was already broken up and gone. Even if she had left Han and gone back, nobody would have trusted a woman who'd been on the road four years enough to marry her. Bad as things were, she had no choice but to stay with Han."

"What is *your* opinion of the incident?"

"You mean whether it was deliberate or an accident?"

"Yes."

"Actually, I've thought a lot about that. But the more I've thought, the more I've come, by degrees, not to understand anything."

"Why is that?"

"I don't know why. I really do not. I think anyone would have the same problem. I asked the introducer what he thought, but he said he didn't know either."

"Well, at the instant it happened, what did you think?"

"I thought: He's murdered her. I did think that."

"Is that so?"

"But the introducer told me that he thought: He's bungled it."

"Is that so? But isn't that what he would think, not knowing too much about their relationship?"

"Maybe so. But later, I thought that my thinking he'd murdered her might also, in the same way, simply have been because I knew a good deal about their relationship."

"What was Han's demeanor just then?"

"He gave a short cry: 'Aa!' That was what drew my attention to what had happened. The blood suddenly gushed out of the wife's neck. Even so, she remained upright for a moment. Her body was held in place by the knife's sticking in the board behind her. Then, all of a sudden, her knees buckled, the knife came out and collapsing all together she fell forward. There was nothing anyone could do. We all of us just went stiff and watched. But I can't be sure of anything. I didn't have the leisure to observe Han's demeanor just then. But it seems to me that for those few seconds he was just like us. It was only afterward that I thought: He's murdered her at last. Han went dead pale and stood there with his eyes closed. We drew the curtain down and tried to revive the woman, but she was already dead. Han, his face bluish with excitement, blurted out: 'How could I make such a blunder?' Then he knelt, in a long silent prayer."

"Was his demeanor agitated then?"

"It was somewhat agitated."

"Good. If I have any further questions, I'll call you."

Dismissing the Chinese stagehand, the judge finally had Han himself brought in. Han, his face drawn and pale, was an intelligent-looking man. It was clear at a glance to the judge that he was suffering from nervous exhaustion. As soon as Han had seated himself, the judge said: "I've been questioning the owner-manager and the stagehand. I will now ask you some questions." Han nodded.

"Have you never loved your wife at all?"

"From the day I married her until the day she had the baby, I loved my wife with all my heart."

"Why did the birth become a source of discord?"

"Because I knew it wasn't my child."

"Do you know who the father was?"

"I have an idea it was my wife's cousin."

"Did you know the man?"

"He was a close friend of mine. It was he who suggested that we get married. He introduced me to her."

"Was there a relationship before she married you?"

"Of course there was. The baby was born the eighth month after the marriage."

"The stagehand said it was a premature birth."

"That's because I told him it was."

"The baby died shortly afterwards?"

"Yes."

"What was the cause of death?"

"It choked at the breast."

"Was that a deliberate act of your wife's?"

"She said it was an accident."

The judge, falling silent, looked intently at Han. Han, eyes lowered in his raised face, waited for the next question.

"Did your wife tell you about the relationship?"

"No, she didn't. Nor did I ask her about it. I felt that the baby's death was a judgement on her for what she'd done. I thought that I myself should be as forgiving as possible."

"But, in the end, you couldn't forgive her?"

"That's right. My feeling remained that the baby's death wasn't enough of a judgement. At times, when I thought about it by myself, I could be rather forgiving. But then, my wife would come in. She would go about her business. As I looked at her, at her body, I could not keep down my displeasure."

"You didn't think of divorcing her?"

"I often thought I'd like a divorce. But I never said anything."

"Why was that?"

"I was weak. And my wife had said that if I divorced her she would not survive."

"Did your wife love you?"

"She did not love me."

"If that was so, why did she say such a thing?"

"I think it was from the necessity of going on living. Her brother had broken up the household back home, and she knew that no respectable man would marry a woman who'd been the wife of a road-player. And her feet were too small for ordinary work."

"What were your sexual relations?"

"I believe they were probably not much different from those of an average couple."

"Did your wife feel any sympathy for you?"

"I can't think she felt any sympathy. I believe that for my wife living with me was an extraordinary hardship. But the patience with which she endured that hardship was beyond what one would have thought possible even for a man. My wife simply observed, with cruel eyes, the gradual destruction of my life. My writhing, desperate attempts to save myself, to enter upon my true life, she coolly, from the side and without the slightest wish to help, as if surrounding me, looked on at."

"Why were you unable to take a more assertive, resolute attitude?"

"Because I was thinking about various things."

"Various things? What sort of things?"

"I thought I would act in such a way as to leave no room for error. But, in the end, those thoughts never offered any solution."

"Did you ever think of killing your wife?"

Han did not answer. The judge repeated his question. Even then, Han did not answer immediately. Then, he said:

"I'd often thought, before then, that it would be good if she were dead."

"Then, if the law had allowed it, you might have killed her?"

"I was afraid of the law, and I had never had such thoughts before. It was merely because I was weak. But even though I was weak, my desire to live my own life was strong."

"So, after that, you thought about killing your wife?"

"I didn't make my mind up to it. But I did think about it."

"How long before the incident was this?"

"The night before. Toward daybreak."

"Had you quarrelled that evening?"

"Yes."

"What about?"

"Something so trivial it isn't worth mentioning."

"Tell me anyway."

"It was about food. When I'm hungry, I get irritable. The way she dawdled over the preparations for supper made me angry."

"Did you quarrel more violently than usual?"

"No. But I remained excited longer than usual. It was because lately I'd felt intolerably frustrated by the fact that I did not have a life of my own. I went to bed, but I couldn't sleep at all. I thought about all sorts of things. I felt as if my present existence in which, like a grub suspended in midair, I looked to one side and the other, always hesitating, without the courage to want what I wanted, without the courage to get rid of what was unbearable, was all due to my relationship with my wife. I could see no light in my future. A desire to seek the light was burning inside me. Or, if it was not, it was trying to catch fire. But my relationship with my wife would not let it. The flame was not out. It was smouldering, in a fitful, ugly way. What with the pain and unhappiness of it all, I was being poisoned. When the poisoning was complete, I would die. Although alive, I would be a dead man. And though this was what I had come to, I was still trying to put up with it. It would be good if she died—one part of me kept having that dirty, hateful thought. If this was how things were, why didn't I kill her? The consequences of such an act did not trouble me now. I might be put in jail. Who could tell how much better life in jail might be than this life? I would cross that bridge when I came to it. It would be enough if, in any way I could, I broke through whatever came up at the time it came up. Even if I broke through, and broke through, I might not break through all the way. But if I went on breaking through until the day I died, that would be my true life. I almost forgot that my wife was lying beside me. At last, I grew tired. But even though I was tired, it was not the sort of fatigue that leads to sleep. My thoughts began to blur. As my tensed up feelings relaxed, my dark thoughts of murder faded away. A feeling of loneliness came over me, as after a nightmare. I even felt pity for my own weak spirit, that the ability to think hard had, in a single night, become so feeble and forlorn. And then, at last, the night was over. It seemed to me that my wife hadn't slept either."

"When you got up, was everything as usual between you?"

"Neither of us said a word to each other."

"Why didn't you think of leaving your wife?"

"Do you mean that as a desired result, it would have come to the same thing?"

"Yes."

"For me, there was a great difference."

Saying this, Han looked at the judge and was silent. The judge, his face softening, nodded.

"But, between my thinking about such a thing and actually deciding to kill her, there was still a wide gap. That day, from early morning on, I felt insanely keyed up. Because of my bodily fatigue, my nerves were edgy, without elasticity. Unable to remain still, I stayed outside all morning. I walked about restlessly, away from the others. I kept thinking that no matter what I would have to do something. But I no longer thought of killing her, as I had the night before. And I was not at all worried about that day's performance. If I had been, I would not have chosen that particular act. We had many other acts. Finally, that evening, our turn came. Then also, I was not thinking of such a thing. As usual, I demonstrated to the audience that the knives were sharp by slicing through a slice of paper and sticking a knife into the stage. My wife, heavily made up and wearing a gaudy Chinese costume, came on. Her stage manner was no different from always. Greeting the audience with a winsome smile, she stepped up to the thick board and stood bolt upright with her back to it. A knife in my hand, I stood at a set distance straight across from her. For the first time since the night before, we exchanged looks. Only then did I realize the danger of having chosen this act for tonight. Unless I practiced the utmost care, I thought, there would be trouble. I must alleviate, as best I could, the day's restless agitation and my strained, edgy nerves. But no matter how I tried, a weariness that had eaten into my heart would not let me. I began to feel that I could not trust my own arm. Closing my eyes, I attempted to calm myself. My body started to sway. The moment came. I drove in the first knife above her head. It went in slightly higher than usual. Then I drove in one knife each under the pits of her arms which were raised to shoulder level. As each knife left my fingertips, something clung to it an instant, as if to hold it back. I felt as if I no longer knew where the knives would go in. Each time one hit, I thought: Thank God. Calm down, calm down, I thought. But I could feel in my arm the constraint that comes from a thing's having become conscious. I drove in a knife to the left of her throat. I was about to drive in the next one to the right, when suddenly a strange look came over her face. She must have felt an impulse of violent fear. Did she have a premonition that the knife about to fly at her would go through her neck? I don't know. I only felt that face of violent fear, thrown back at my heart with the same force as the knife. Dizziness struck me. But even so, with all my strength, almost without a target, as though aiming in the dark, I threw the knife . . ."

The judge was silent.

"I've killed her at last, I thought."

"How do you mean? That you'd done it on purpose?"

"Yes. I suddenly felt as if I had."

"Afterwards, you knelt by the body in silent prayer . . . ?"

"That was a trick that occurred to me at the moment. I knew everyone thought I seriously believed in Christianity. While pretending to pray, I was thinking about what attitude I should take."

"You felt sure that what you'd done was intentional?"

"Yes. And I thought right away I could make out it was an accident."

"But why did you think it was deliberate murder?"

"Because of my feelings, which were unhinged."

"So you thought you'd skillfully deceived the others?"

"Thinking about it later, I was shocked at myself. I acted surprised in a natural manner, was considerably agitated, and also displayed grief. But any perceptive person, I believe, could have seen that I was playacting. Recalling my behavior, I sweated cold sweat. That night, I decided that I would have to be found innocent. First of all, I was extremely encouraged by the fact that there was not a scrap of objective proof of my crime. Everyone knew we'd been on bad terms, of course, so there was bound to be a suspicion of murder. I couldn't do anything about that. But if I insisted, throughout, that it was an accident, that would be the end of it. That we'd gotten along badly might make people conjecture, but it was no proof. In the end, I thought, I would be acquitted for lack of evidence. Thinking back over the incident, I made up a rough version of my plea, as plausible as possible, so that it would seem like an accident. Soon, though, for some reason, a doubt rose up in me as to whether I myself believed it was murder. The night before, I had thought about killing her, but was that alone a reason for deciding, myself, that it was murder? Gradually, despite myself, I became unsure. A sudden excitement swept over me. I felt so excited I couldn't sit still. I was so happy, I was beside myself. I wanted to shout for joy."

"Was it because you yourself could now believe that it was an accident?"

"No. I'm still unsure of that. It was because it was completely unclear, even to myself, which it had been. It was because I could now tell the truth and be found innocent. Being found innocent meant everything to me now. For that purpose, rather than trying to deceive myself and insisting that it was an accident, it was far better to be able to be honest, even if it meant saying I didn't know which it was. I could no longer assert that it was an accident, nor, on the other hand, could I say that it was a deliberate act. I was so happy because come what may it was no longer a question of a confession of guilt."

Han fell silent. The judge, also, was silent for a moment. Then, as if to himself, he said: "On the whole, it seems to be the truth." And then: "By the way, do you not feel the slightest sorrow about your wife's death?"

"None whatsoever. And up to now, no matter what my feelings of hatred for her, I never imagined that I'd be able to talk so cheerfully about her death."

"That will be all. You may step down," the judge said. Han, after a slight wordless bow, left the room.

The judge felt an excitement, he could not put a name to it, surge up in him.

Quickly, he took up his pen. And, then and there, he wrote: "Innocent."

✲

✲

At Kinosaki

✲

I was struck and thrown to the ground by a trolley car of the Yamanote line. To recuperate from my injury, I went by myself to a hot springs inn at Kinosaki in Tajima. If the injury to my back should develop into spinal tuberculosis, it might prove fatal. But I was told by the doctor that that kind of thing was not at all likely. If nothing happened in two or three years, I would not have anything to worry about afterwards. In the meantime, I was told, it was important that I take good care of myself. So I had come here. I intended to stay more than three weeks—if I could stand it, for five weeks.

I was still not quite clear in my head. My forgetfulness became acute. But my mood was calm as it had not been in recent years. I had a nice, quiet feeling. It was the beginning of the rice harvest, and the weather also was fine.

I was all alone. There was no one to talk to. I spent the day reading and writing, or sat in a chair outside my room vaguely looking at the mountains or the road, or else took walks. A good place for walking was the road that went up from the town by slow degrees alongside a small stream. There was a little pool at a bend in the stream around the foot of the mountain where trout congregated. If you looked more closely, you might discover big freshwater crabs with hairs on their claws sitting as still as stones. I often walked on this road before supper. As I went up along the small, clear stream through the lonely autumn ravine in the chilly evening, my thoughts were often of unhappy things. They were lonely thoughts. But in them there was this nice quiet feeling. I often thought about my accident. An inch or two either way, I thought, and I would now be face up under the sod in the graveyard at Aoyama. With a pale, cold, stiff face, the cuts on it and on my back just as they were. The bodies of my grandfather and my mother would be by my side. And yet, there would no longer be any communication between us—such were the thoughts I had. Although they were lonely thoughts, they did not disquiet me all that much. Death would come sooner or later. Up until now, in my thoughts, I had pretty much assumed that it would be much later, in the far distant future. But now I felt that I truly did not know when it would come. In a book about the life of Lord Clive, which I read in middle school, it was written that Clive was encouraged by thinking to himself that there was something that had saved him from a likely death, had kept him alive for a work that he had to do. That was the way that I wanted to feel about my own brush with death. And I did have such a feeling. But in the end my heart was curiously quiescent. Something like an affection for death arose within me.

My room, being the only room on the second floor, was comparatively quiet. When I grew tired of reading and writing, I often went out to the chair on the veranda. Alongside me was the roof of the downstairs entryway. There was a wainscoting where it was joined to the house. Evidently there was a wasps' nest in that wainscot. Every day, as long as the weather held, the corpulent tiger-striped wasps were out hard at work from morning almost until nightfall. When they emerged, brushing the sides of the loosely joined planks of the paneling, the wasps would descend to the roof of the entryway for a while. There they would meticulously adjust their wings and antennae with their front and back legs. Then they would walk about a bit. All of a sudden, their slender wings stretched taut to either side, they lifted off with a resonant buzz. When they'd flown up like that, they suddenly shot away into the distance. The flowers of the yatsude being in bloom just then, the wasps clustered about its shrubbery. When I was bored, I would often watch the comings and goings of the wasps from the veranda railing.

One morning, I spotted a wasp that had died on the roof of the entryway. Its legs tucked tightly under its stomach, its feelers were drooped untidily over its face. The other wasps were perfectly indifferent to it. Although they busily crawled around it on their way in and out of the nest, they showed no signs of being otherwise affected by it. Certainly the wasps, as they went indefatigably about their work, gave you an impression of the living creature. And the one wasp by their side, which morning, noon, and night was always in the same place whenever I looked, absolutely still, tumbled over on its face, just as surely gave the feeling of something that had died. It stayed that way for about three days. Looking at it gave me such a feeling of quietness. It was lonely. In the evening, when all the other wasps had gone inside the nest, it was lonely to see that one little corpse remaining outside on the cold roof tiles. But what a quiet feeling it was.

During the night, there was a heavy rainfall. In the morning, it was clear again. The leaves, the surface of the ground, and the roof were all washed beautifully clean. The wasp's body was no longer in its place. Already the wasps from the nest were energetically at work. Probably the dead wasp had been washed down through the eaves' gutter to the ground. With its legs shrivelled up and its feelers stuck to its face, covered with mud, it was probably lying still as a pebble somewhere. Until the next change in its surroundings that would move it occurred, the little corpse would most likely stay where it was. Or would it be dragged away by ants? Whatever, it was certainly quiet. It was quiet because a wasp that had been nothing but busy, busy had become absolutely still. I felt an intimacy in that stillness. A short while before, I had written a short story called "Han's Crime." From jealousy of an old premarital relationship between his wife and a man who was his friend, also driven by his own psychological pressures, a Chinese called Han had murdered his wife. As I had written the story, it was mainly about Han's feelings. Now, however, I thought of writing a story about the feelings of his wife. Murdered at the end, under the ground of the cemetery—I wanted to write about that quietness of hers.

I thought I would write "The Murdered Wife of Han." I did not write the story after all, but the need for it had arisen in me. It was a feeling that differed greatly from the thoughts of the hero of a long story that I'd been working on before. I was at a loss.

It was shortly after the wasp's body had been washed away, removed from my field of vision. One morning, thinking I'd go to Mount Higashi Park with its view of the Maruyama River and the Sea of Japan into which it emptied, I left the inn. From in front of a hot spring called Ichi-no-yu, a small stream flowed gently down the middle of the road and entered the Maruyama River. When I came to a certain place, the bridge and sides of the stream were lined with people. They were having a good time watching something in the brook. What they were looking at was a big rat that had been tossed into the water. Desperately swimming, the rat was trying to get away. The rat's neck had been pierced with a fish skewer about eight inches in length. Three inches or so of it stuck out behind the head, and three inches or so stuck out from the throat. The rat was trying to climb up on the stone embankment. Two or three children and a rickshawman of about forty were chucking stones at it. Their aim wasn't very good. With a clattering noise, the stones bounced back off the embankment. The onlookers were laughing loudly. The rat finally got a toehold between the stones of the embankment. But when it tried to climb up, the skewer immediately got in its way. And so it dropped back into the water. The rat was trying to rescue itself somehow. A human being could not understand the expression of its face, but it was clear from its actions that it was trying very hard. As if thinking that if it could just get away somewhere it would be safe, still transfixed by the long skewer, the rat began to swim out toward the middle of the stream. Having more fun than ever, the children and the rickshawman threw their stones. Two or three domestic ducks, which had been foraging for food in front of a laundry stone to the side, were startled by the flying stones and craned their necks, goggle-eyed. The stones hit the water with a swift plunking sound. The ducks, their necks still stretched out, with silly expressions of dismay and squawks of alarm, made their way upstream with busily paddling feet. I had no heart to watch the rat's last moments. The appearance of the rat as it fled for its life with all its strength, laboring under a fate that would end in death, remained strangely in my mind. I had a lonely, unpleasant feeling. That was the truth, I thought to myself. Before the quietness that I aspired toward, there was that terrible suffering. I might have an affection for the quietness after death, but until I achieved that death I would likely have a dreadful time of it. Creatures that did not know of suicide had to continue their efforts until they had finally done dying. If I were in a situation similar to the rat's, what would I do? Wouldn't I struggle, as the rat had done? I could not but think of the time of my accident, when I was close to death. I had tried to do everything that was possible. I had decided myself on the hospital. I had designated the way to go there. Thinking that if the doctor were out, it would be inconvenient if the preparations for surgery were not ready upon my arrival, I requested that somebody phone ahead. Afterward, it had seemed strange even to me that in a half-conscious state my mind had worked well on the most important things. The question of whether the injury was fatal or not was literally a matter of life and death. Even so, I was almost completely unassailed by the fear of death. This also seemed strange to me. "Is it fatal or not? What did the doctor say?" I asked a friend who was standing by. "He says it's not a fatal injury," I was told. This answer cheered me up immediately. From excitement, I became extraordinarily happy. How would I have acted if I'd been told: "It's fatal"? I could not at all imagine myself in such a case. Probably I would have felt sad. But I had the feeling that I would not have been attacked by the fear with which one usually thinks of death. I had the feeling that even if I had been told I was dying, I would have thought all the more of doing something to save myself. Doubtless I would not have been so different in that from the rat. Trying to imagine how it would be if I'd had my accident now, I thought that probably it would be much the same thing. Doubtless what I hoped for would have no very immediate effect on how it was for me. And either way was all right. It was all right with me whether my hopes influenced my condition or not. There was nothing I could do about it.

Some time after this incident, I slowly made my way up along the little stream from the town one evening. When I crossed the tracks in front of the tunnel of the Yamakage line, the road became narrow and steep. The stream also became steep, and swift. There were no houses at all around here. Thinking to myself that I would turn back, I kept walking "until that place up there," on and on, around bend after bend. Everything was pale and faint. The air was cold on my skin. Oddly, the quietness somehow made me nervous. There was a big mulberry tree by the roadside. On the far side of the tree, on a branch that stretched out over the road, a single leaf was fluttering the same way again and again. There was no wind, and aside from the stream everything was quiet. In the midst of all that silence and stillness, the one solitary leaf was continually and agitatedly aflutter. It struck me as peculiar. I even felt slightly afraid. But I was also curious. Going down under the tree, I looked up at that leaf for a while. Then, the wind began to blow. And as it did so, the moving leaf became still. The cause was evident. I thought that somehow I could understand such things better now.

It was gradually growing dark. No matter how far I went, there was always another turning. I'll turn back here, I thought. Casually, I looked at the stream off to the side. On the slope of the far bank, on a flat rock, about half the size of a tatami mat, that stood out of the water, there was a small black creature. It was a water lizard. Still wet, it had a beautiful color. Its head lower, it faced the stream stilly from the slant rock. It did not move. The water that dripped from its body trickled about an inch down the dark dry stone. I squatted down at ease and watched it. I was not as averse to water lizards as I once had been. I felt some liking for ordinary lizards. The lizards known as "shrine guardians" I detested above all others. As for water lizards, I neither liked nor disliked them. About ten years earlier, at Ashi-no-Mizu-umi, I'd often watched the water lizards gather around the spout where the wastewater from the inn ran off. I often got the feeling that it would be unbearable to be a water lizard. I thought of such things as what I would do if I was reborn as a water lizard. Since at that time I had such thoughts when I saw the water lizards, I'd disliked looking at them. But now I no longer thought about such things. I thought I'd try to startle the water lizard and make him go into the water. I remembered the way they walked, clumsily swinging their bodies. Still squatting, I picked up a stone the size of a small ball that was by me and threw it. I wasn't particularly aiming at the lizard. I am so bad at taking aim and throwing something that even when I do my best I come nowhere near the mark. I never thought that I would hit the lizard. After a clunking sound, the stone fell into the stream. Simultaneously with the sound, the lizard seemed to have leapt sideways about four inches. Arching its tail, the lizard held it up high. I wondered what had happened. It did not occur to me at first that the stone had hit it. Quietly, of its own accord, the warped tail of the lizard came down. Squaring its elbows against the slope of the rock, the lizard, the toes of its forefeet braced in front of it curling inward, weakly tumbled forward. Its tail clung to the rock. It was motionless. The water lizard was dead. You've done a terrible thing, I thought. I had often killed insects and the like. But the fact that I had killed the lizard without at all meaning to pierced me with a strange unpleasantness. It was something I had done, of course, but it was absolutely fortuitous. For the lizard, it was a totally unexpected death. I squatted there for some time. With the feeling that it was me and the lizard now, I became as the lizard. I lived that feeling. I felt it was piteous, and at the same time I felt the loneliness of all life. By chance I had not died. By chance the lizard had died. With a lonely feeling, I came back down the road, which I could hardly see in front of my feet, toward the inn. Distantly, the lights at the edge of the town began to appear. What had become of the dead wasp? Probably later rains had buried it under the earth already. What had happened to that rat? Perhaps about this time, having been carried out to sea, its water-bloated corpse was being washed up on the beach together with some garbage. And I, who had not died, was walking along in this way. That was what I thought. I felt that it would not do for me not to be thankful. But in actual fact, no feeling of gratitude came welling up in me. Being alive and dying were not positive and negative poles. I had the feeling that there was not that much difference between them. It was quite dark by now. I merely felt that the distant lights were there. The sensation of walking separated from the sense of sight. It was very uncertain going. Only my mind went on willfully working. It drew me all the more into such a mood.

After staying for about three weeks, I left that place. Already more than three years have gone by since then. I did not come down with spinal tuberculosis. That much at least I was spared.

✲

✲

Akanishi Kakita

✲

In the old days, in the mansion of Daté Hyobu on the Sendai Slope, there was a newly arrived samurai retainer by the name of Akanishi Kakita. Although said to be thirty four or -five years old, he was old for his age and looked over forty. His features were of the so-called ugly man type, and he had an uncouth accent. In every respect, he seemed the typical back-country samurai. His speech being unlike the Sendai speech, he was thought to be from Akita or thereabouts, but actually had been born in Matsué of Unshu. A conscientious, solitary hard worker, in general he had a good reputation. But he did not seem to have a very commanding personality. The smart young samurai, using him for one thing and another, made a fool of him. Kakita calmly allowed them to do it. But the young samurai were no fools themselves, and it was not pleasant for them to feel that their not overly charming thoughts were seen through by this Kakita who let himself be used. After a while, they stopped.

Kakita, being single, lived without a servant in one room of the samurai longhouse. Since he neither drank nor dallied with women, it was thought that he must have trouble killing time off duty. But Kakita was not all that bored. Instead of drinking saké, he ate a lot of sweets. Whenever the sweets vendor, with his shoulder pack of shallow boxes piled atop each other and tied with a Sanada braid rope, came where Kakita happened to be, he never failed to make a sale. Even in buying sweets, though, Kakita's unattractive quirkiness came to the surface. After he'd asked the prices of everything, he would agitate his fingers like chopsticks over the sweets. The vendor would think: "I've brought pretty much the same things, but he still doesn't remember the prices." On days when he was in a bad mood, he would get very angry. But Kakita, even if he did remember, was not satisfied until he'd asked at least once.

Moreover, Kakita, the lover of sweets, had stomach and intestinal problems. If there was an unfailing supply of sweets in his room, there was also an unfailing supply of the medicinal herb *senburi*. Its scent always hovered in his room.

Besides sweets, Kakita had one other diversion. This was chess, at which he was surprisingly good. He who was tightfisted when buying sweets startled his opponents by his rather openhanded moves. As there was something sharp in his way of doing this, it often seemed extremely unsporting. But Kakita did not desire opponents so much as he simply liked to play. An open rule book on his lap, he liked to set up the pieces by himself. Placing a paper lantern across the board, he often played against himself until late at night. At a glance, he seemed to be playing against the lantern. Some of his colleagues teased him about this. "How did the game with the lantern turn out last night?" they might say.

In the Sendai mansion of Harada Kai at Atagoshita, there was a young samurai-retainer by the name of Ginzamé Masujiro. A lively, intelligent, good-looking man, he liked to drink and enjoyed women. In general, his tastes and behavior were the opposite of Kakita's. The two men were the same, however, in their love of chess.

Since their chance meeting when Kakita had gone on an errand for his lord to Atagoshita, the two had become strange and great friends as chess partners.

When they saw how two such different men had become boon companions, people remarked that there was no accounting for taste. But nobody found it that peculiar or indeed anything of the kind.

A year went by uneventfully. Every ten or fifteen days, the two went back and forth as usual and engaged each other in chess matches.

Later on, a curious rumor sprang up about Kakita. It was said that he had tried to commit suicide. Sure enough, when people went to see, Kakita had been lying face up and semiconscious, more dead than alive. Even his friend Masujiro, who sat by his side, did not know why he had done such a thing. When they asked the doctor, he said that Kakita had actually stitched up his own abdomen with upwards of ten acupuncture needles.

"He has stomach trouble. He must have been dreaming and done it to himself when he was half asleep, the fool," somebody said. "Maybe he's crazy," somebody else said.

One night, in the room of the elder lady-in-waiting Ezo Chrysanthemum, a masseur called Anko had divulged the true story of the failed suicide. The facts were as follows:

Summoned to Kakita's room that night, Anko had found him curled up in agony like a shrimp. "My stomach is killing me. Massage me or give me acupuncture, quick," Kakita commanded him. Anko immediately put in five or six needles, but Kakita, in evident torment, said it was no help at all. Thinking it must be a stomach cramp, Anko put in some needles in the area of the solar plexus. After five or six of these, however, Kakita said: "The pain is farther down." When Anko asked: "Here?" he said it was more to the right. When Anko pressed his right side, he said it was more to the left. Then he said: "Anywhere's all right. Massage all around there, as hard as you can." Presently, Anko began massaging the abdomen. Somehow it was strangely swollen. This was not a job for him, Anko thought. Kakita grew angry. "It's no good unless you do it with all your strength." "Abdominal massage isn't something you put that much strength into," Anko replied. "If intestinal torsion results, it's the end."

"Intestinal torsion? What's that?" Kakita asked. "It's when your insides get all twisted up." Saying this, Anko put a little more strength into his massage. But what was happening? The abdomen was becoming more and more swollen. Suddenly, Kakita turned dead pale. Each time he drew breath, he gave a strange cry of pain. "Aaa . . . aa . . . aaa . . . aa!" Anko was horrified. In his younger days (telling the story to Ezo Chrysanthemum, he left out only this), he'd given an inexpert massage and killed a man by intestinal torsion. When Anko went to see him the day after the massage, the man's appearance had been no different from Kakita's now. There was nothing to do but call a doctor, Anko thought. Even so, he felt helpless and downcast. "Something is terribly wrong. I don't know if I did it, or if it happened before I touched him, but nobody's going to ask me for a massage after this," Anko anxiously thought to himself. Timidly, he said: "Please call in a doctor." "It must be intestinal torsion," Kakita replied tormentedly. "It does seem that way." Then Kakita, with a frightful visage, glared at Anko. Anko was astonished. But then, Kakita quietly said, "Whatever it is, tell me the truth." Anko bowed his head. "Yes." "A doctor could do nothing about this." Anko could not bring himself to say "Yes" again. So he said nothing . . .

Having got this far, the loquacious masseur Anko abruptly fell silent. Then, in an unaccountably agitated manner, he completed his story in very abbreviated form. In short, Kakita, saying, "Well now, if it's a hopeless case," had cut himself open. Making Anko help, he'd put his intestines back in order. (At this point, you may say, the old lady-in-waiting, if she'd had the slightest smattering of medical knowledge, surely would have asked: "But how did they control the bleeding?" Unfortunately, however, she hadn't possessed such knowledge. Even if she had, the old lady might simply have been dumbstruck at Kakita's courage and unable to raise the question just then. As you will discover if you read on, Kakita, despite even peritonitis, somehow survived.)

"I have never seen a man of such powerful will," Anko concluded. "But I am sworn to secrecy in the matter. Please do not tell anyone." Repeating this request again and again, he took his leave of the old lady.

It was a morning two or three days afterward. At the base of the Sendai Slope lay the corpse of Anko the masseur. He had been cut down with a single sword-stroke to the neck, from behind.

It was an afternoon two or three days after that. At the pillow of Kakita, who had made good progress and was already able to talk a little, sat Masujiro.

Kakita, from his bed where he lay on his back, looked up into Masujiro's face. In a weak voice, he said:

"It was you who killed Anko, wasn't it?"

"Not I," replied Masujiro, with a disagreeable smile.

"I feel sorry for the poor fellow." Saying this, Kakita languidly closed his eyes again.

In another week, when Masujiro went to see him, Kakita was much stronger. They began to chat about the incident.

"You're a fool. Why did you tell a gossip monger like Anko the whereabouts of the secret report?" Smilingly, Masujiro chided Kakita.

"Please don't talk that way. Death is the same for all of us. Even a dog's death is painful. What I cannot atone for, even by death, is having let the report to the Lord of Shiroishi, nearly two years in the writing, rot in the ceiling with mouse-scat."

"Maybe so, but why did you tell Anko, of all people?"

"Whom else could I have told?"

"Did you have to tell anyone? There would have been no slipup. As soon as I'd heard of your death, I would have come on the run. I would have found a chance to look for it."

"Even now, do you have any idea where and how it's hidden?"

"Idea, nothing—that masseur gave me detailed instructions.

Soon after you began to get better, he told me everything. First he looked secretive, and then triumphant. He really ran off at the mouth. I had the feeling that if I let him live he was sure to noise it abroad and soon. Well, anyway, I took care of him. Even if you had died, and he'd brought me the document as you'd told him to, I could not have let him live."

"That may be so."

"You say that, but even now you don't think so. But if you had died, I would surely have thought that you'd sent him to me to be killed."

"I never intended such a thing. I trusted him to some extent. I knew he was a gossip, but I thought he would keep the secret until our duty was done. Because it was my last request."

"Still the man of noble character, eh?" Masujiro made a slight grimace.

Kakita was silent.

Masujiro, though, was not the sort who could hold his tongue at a time like this.

"It hurts even you. You were nearly killed by him, and you're still defending him."

"I had the intestinal torsion long before the massage. The doctor told me that. It didn't suddenly happen as he was massaging me."

"But his clumsy technique must soon have made matters worse."

Again, Kakita was silent. Masujiro also, this time, said nothing. But after a while, he spoke again.

"Be that as it may, we have by and large accomplished our duty. When you're strong enough, we should return to Shiroishi at the first good opportunity."

"Yes. Let's do that."

Two months passed. It was the day of the autumnal equinox. Kakita was already fully recovered. Masujiro being off duty that day, the two rented a boat in the landfill district and went fishing for gobies. Kakita had brought sweets with his lunch, and Masujiro saké with his. Along the stone embankment of Ohama Castle, the two caught a lot of fish. But there were many boats nearby, and they could not talk freely.

"How about it? We've already caught enough. Why don't we go out a little farther and have our lunches where we can be alone?" Masujiro began to wind in the several lines dangling from his pole.

"Yes. Let's," Kakita replied, also raising his pole.

"That tall round mountain over there must be Mt. Kano."

"Oh?"

"This kind of scenery gives the saké a special taste. But it's no good with you munching away on your sweets."

Kakita merely smiled.

"Even with sweets, though, you can have too many. What kind have you brought today? If they're too rich, they're probably bad for you."

"Today, I brought some wafers."

"You're just like a baby." Masujiro let out a loud laugh.

When they'd stowed their tackle, Masujiro rowed out toward the open water. Coming alongside the channel stakes, he moored the boat to one. There were no other boats around. With a sense of pleasant relaxation, each man opened his lunch box.

"Do you feel strong enough to travel yet?" Masujiro asked.

"I'm just about ready."

"The rowing didn't tire you?"

"Not especially."

"If that's so, why don't we make preparations to return to Shiroishi before long? My own report is more or less complete."

"In that case, you should go back ahead. I'm also more or less done, but . . ."

"Shouldn't we wait a while, until Kai arrives?"

"Yes, perhaps."

"Anyway, when you've set your day of departure, I'll leave a little ahead of you."

"That's all right, but what reason can I give for taking a leave of absence?"

"It won't do if objections are raised when you make your formal request."

"Should I make a getaway by night, then? But that, too, may be risky unless it's for some reason they can understand. And it would be dangerous for you if you were left behind."

"Well, Kai is an intelligent man. We mustn't make a false move and give the other side an advantage. But how would your night getaway seem the most natural?"

Kakita, not thinking this kind of elaborate tactics was his business, left everything up to Masujiro without trying to ponder on the matter.

"It will have to be because of something dishonorable. Something after which you won't be able to face people," Masujiro said, with an unpleasant grin.

"You mean I'll disgrace the name of samurai?"

"Yes, you'll disgrace the name of samurai," repeated Masujiro gleefully.

"You're not asking me to commit a theft, surely?"

"A theft might be just the thing."

"But they'd catch me as soon as they started chasing me."

"A chase would be good, but you're right, they'd catch you before you'd stolen anything."

The two men laughed.

Kakita quietly ate his lunch. Masujiro, nibbling on tidbits, sipping saké, gazing at the panoramic scenery, was deep in thought.

"How's this?" Abruptly striking his knee, Masujiro spoke excitedly. "You'll write a love letter to somebody. All right? The more refined and beautiful she is, the better. You'll send her a note. It's too bad, but you'll be turned down. You'll be a laughingstock. Your honor will have been trampled on, so you won't be able to remain in the castle. You'll have to flee at night. Isn't that a good plan? With a face like yours, it's bound to succeed.

Let's see now, who could be your lady love? Someone like a lady-in-waiting. An old woman is no good. She'd be shameless in her curiosity. It's got to be an elegant young woman."

Masujiro said the most absurd things, Kakita thought. But he did not get angry. Unenthusiastically, he replied:

"It may be better than committing theft."

"What do you mean, better? It's the best idea in the world. There must be someone we can think of. I know you don't usually go in for that sort of thing, but . . ."

Kakita did not answer.

"There must be some woman the young men all talk about."

"There *is* a very beautiful lady-in-waiting, called Sazaé."

"Sazaé, eh? So even you don't mind laying your eyes on her. Well, if it's Sazaé, it's sure to work."

Hitherto, Kakita had not felt any emotion of love toward Sazaé. But he was well aware of her beauty. And he knew that hers was a clean beauty. Although sending her a love letter would be a stratagem with another, serious purpose, it did not seem right. It frightened him.

"Let's make it some other lady-in-waiting. Not Sazaé."

"Don't get mushy over her, now. It won't do." Masujiro was no longer joking. What he meant by "get mushy" was unclear to Kakita, but he felt sure that sending such a letter to Sazaé was entirely inappropriate and furthermore like sullying a perfect thing. He did not want to do it. But if a young, lovely woman was necessary for the success Masujiro spoke of, he himself could not think of anyone except Sazaé. Resigning himself, he agreed to make Sazaé the recipient.

"Write me a draft of the letter, then."

"No. You'll have to write it yourself. If I wrote it, it would be my love letter. Since the lady is Sazaé, she might like it all too much. I could make her fall for me just like that."

Kakita forced a smile. The thought came to him that if he, rather than Masujiro, wrote the letter, he might manage not to defile Sazaé.

A wind having sprung up, the two took the boat in. Since it was on his way, Kakita accompanied Masujiro to the mansion at Atagoshita. There, for the first time in many weeks, they had a game of chess.

Autumn came. It was the first definitely chilly evening. Kakita, warming his hands at a meager banked fire in the brazier in his quiet room, spread out a roll of cheap writing paper and thought hard. Now and then, his face intensely serious, he scratched the shaven part of his head with the hand holding the pen, as if at a loss.

Finally, he started writing.

It did not go well at all. The calligraphy was first-rate, but the contents were no good. Curiously solemn, the letter had neither charm nor taste. "This is no kind of love letter," Kakita thought, smiling bitterly to himself.

He tried thinking back to stories he had read, but couldn't particularly recall any passages about love letters. Then he tried to think of himself as a handsome young samurai of twenty or so, such as he'd seen in storybook pictures. It was not that he didn't get some of the feeling, but when he opened his eyes there was his dark, hairy, clumsy hand. He was stumped.

He began to have other doubts. Perhaps it would be easier to write to a different woman. Or perhaps he should give up the idea of the letter and speak to Sazaé directly. But that might be even more difficult, he thought. He should have left the writing of the letter to Masujiro.

Also, as he imagined Sazaé's surprise and displeasure when she received the letter, his heart sank. Pulling himself together, he began again to write. But it was quite unsatisfactory—altogether too brisk and businesslike. It didn't sound at all as if he were in the throes of love. He was completely stuck.

At any rate, it was a mistake to think of it as a love letter. Instead of making something up, he should write so as to reveal his true self. With this thought, he tried to lure himself into the feeling that he was in love with Sazaé. He tried to become a Kakita who was languishing in the flames of passion for her. To some extent, he succeeded. Hastily, before the feeling wore off, he propelled his pen along the paper. Even so, in a little while, when he woke up from the feeling, he was at his wit's end again. But one way or another, out of the sympathy he felt for himself as an ugly, pathetic fellow, a kind of love letter emerged with real emotion in it. I cannot write more than this, he thought. Reading it over, he carefully rolled it up and sealed it. As if it were an important document, he stored it away in a drawer, and got ready for bed.

The next morning, Kakita went to the palace earlier than usual. Inconspicuously loitering in the long corridor, he waited for Sazaé. He felt weirdly keyed up. Even though he tried to calm himself, he did not know how to begin. When Sazaé would appear, any minute now, he must not let this chance to hand her the letter slip by. His hand clutching the letter held hidden in a fold of his formal divided skirt, Kakita waited. He was aware that his hand's oily sweat had soaked into the letter.

He felt feeble, as if Sazaé were a formidable opponent. Telling himself this wouldn't do, he tried to concentrate on his duty as a samurai. But he could not help feeling that beautiful Sazaé was the strong party and that he, ugly Kakita, was incomparably the weaker party. He felt very deeply that, between men and women, beauty and ugliness were the same as strength and weakness. The feeling oppressed him. Restlessly, he stepped inside an empty room along the corridor, and stepped out again.

At last, the moment came. His heart pounded. But then, despite everything, he felt oddly composed, not at all like a man tendering a love letter.

"Please read this." With a stern face, and looking straight at Sazaé, he handed her the letter.

Sazaé seemed somewhat taken aback. But then, accepting the letter, she said:

"Is an answer required?" Although he'd never supposed there would be an answer, Kakita replied:

"If you please."

Bowing to him, Sazae went on her way. Kakita gave a great sigh of relief. Well, I did it, he told himself. He felt a sort of good cheer.

Would something happen that same day? Or the next? Wondering, Kakita made his preparations for flight. But nothing happened that day.

The next day came. Since he did not expect an answer, Kakita did not particularly seek an opportunity to receive one. But when that day also passed without incident, he thought: This is strange. He was afraid that Sazae, not wishing to shame him, would cover up the letter as if she'd never gotten it. Sazae was strong-minded beyond her years, and if this was what she'd done, he was in trouble.

The third day went by. There was no opportunity to meet Sazae alone. Afterwards, Kakita realized that without knowing it he'd avoided such a meeting. When they met in the presence of others, she had had the look of one for whom nothing is amiss. In his heart, Kakita admired her for it. But he could not leave things this way. Although he sympathized with her, he would have to write another love letter and drop it somewhere where she would find it.

That night, he wrote the letter. To avoid inconveniencing Sazae as much as possible, he wrote it with great care. In your not having answered my letter, I recognize your kindness, your wish not to shame me. Even I feel it is unforgivable to presume further upon your magnanimity. But I cannot help myself, etc. This was the sort of letter it was. When he thought of some young samurai finding it and bursting into laughter as he read it, Kakita broke out in a cold sweat . . .

The next day, when he reported for duty, Kakita dropped the letter by a wire-netted lantern right at the turning of the corridor.

An hour later, he contrived to go by there. The letter was

already gone. As, with a strange, mingled feeling of relief and unhappiness, he retraced his steps, he happened to meet Sazaé coming from the other direction. When, involuntarily lowering his eyes, he tried to get by her without incident, something touched his hand. Before he was aware, he'd taken it. It was a bulky letter.

That evening, when he got back to his room, he turned up the lamp wick and quickly opened the letter. Her answer was a complete surprise. There were two letters, the second written after coming back with the first one which she had not had the chance to hand to him.

The contents of the first letter were as follows:

I have never been in love with you, but I have always felt friendship for you. Although knowing that before long the question of marriage would arise, I have felt no such inclination toward any of the young samurai that one sees in this castle. It goes without saying that I never thought of such a thing in connection with you. I know you will not take this in an unfavorable sense.

I am the daughter of a merchant. In another year or eighteen months, I am to return to my parents. I have thought that it was my lot after all to marry into a merchant's family. But when I received your letter, a new question arose. As I thought about it, a new emotion welled up in me. I had always felt a certain respect for you. Now, that feeling suddenly crystallized. For the first time, I realized that what without clearly knowing it I'd been searching for was to be found in you. I came to understand that my having been somehow dissatisfied with the so-called handsome young samurai was because that something was not in them. Since I read your letter, truly for the first time I have known what I was looking for. I am happy now.

For the rest, you are displaying a cautiousness which doesn't suit you. I don't take it amiss, but it really serves no purpose. Please don't write that way again. I think of you with happiness from my heart," etc.

The calligraphy of this letter betrayed an ever more beautiful, alluring, womanly passion.

In the second letter, she expressed her regret and incomprehension that he'd not sought out an opportunity to receive her reply. Instructions followed on what they should do in the future. She was thinking of confiding the matter to her parents on her day of leave, which was due soon.

Kakita flushed crimson. He could hear his heart pounding. For a while, he sat in a daze. He did not even know if he should take these letters at face value. A strange emotion, not there five minutes ago, surged freshly into his heart. He forgot how old he was. Kakita had had this feeling only once before, as a lad of twelve or thirteen in his native village of Matsué in Unshu. That time, it had ended in miserable disillusionment, with the scornful smiles of the girl. Since then, he had lost all confidence in himself—as he would have put it, he knew himself. To this day, such an emotion had not come into his heart again.

He felt as if he were in a dream. Presently, though, he was jolted out of it by the memory of the letter he had dropped today. What should he do? This was more than he could cope with. What a fool he was, he thought. Although there was a justification in the motive, he had irresponsibly used another person's purest feelings. How had he forgotten to respect such feelings? How was he to make amends? He thought feverishly.

The night grew late. He went to bed, but he could not sleep. He still had a sense of wonder that things should have turned out this way. It was already too late, he thought. The letter he had dropped would lead to some unknown solution, and he would have to follow it there.

Gradually, his feelings calmed down. His thoughts once again reverted to his duty as a samurai. He felt as if he'd awakened from the dream. It would not do, he thought, to be immersed in his own affairs at this crucial hour when the fate of the country hung in the scales. Now was the hour when he must make his heart into a devil. Come what may, he had to do his duty. Afterwards, Sazae would understand. When everything had turned out well, he could renew their relationship. By then, all would be understood. Though thinking so, Kakita felt a residue of loneliness. After a while, still feeling lonely, he fell asleep.

Morning came. Kakita reported for duty at the regular time. His face was paler than usual. He felt somehow dejected, and also somehow agitated.

After a while, a messenger came from Ezo Chrysanthemum, asking him to come to her room for a moment. Kakita went with a heavy heart. Feeling this was no more than what he deserved, he did not try to put on a brave face.

The old lady, after dismissing her attendants, handed him his own letter.

"It was I who found it, so you're safe. But what would you have done if someone else had found it?" the old lady said, as if upbraiding him.

But even though she spoke that way, she was well-disposed toward Kakita. Particularly since his failed suicide, she had been more and more impressed with this samurai. She sincerely thought it was a pity that he should be injured by this kind of affair. She would not breathe a word of this to anyone, she said. He must carry on as before, as if nothing had happened. As for the other letters, she would retrieve them from Sazae at a good opportunity. More and more earnestly, she admonished him on his future.

Kakita did not say anything. He did not realize how his own good character was being reflected in other people's hearts. How was it that they were all such good people? Although their lord, Hyobu, was evil, when he thought that he must labor to bring down this house in which such good people lived, Kakita felt a faint loneliness.

Pleading illness, Kakita returned to his room. Since things had gone this far, there was nothing to do but carry on to the end. He wrote the following letter to Ezo Chrysanthemum.

It is a shameful thing that, not mindful of my age, I have fallen madly in love. How could I have the face to see you again? I cannot forget the lady Sazaé nor can I perform my duty as before. Truly I have exhausted all claims upon your compassion.

After penning this, he took his own and Masujiro's secret reports from their hiding place in the ceiling and put them under his clothes next to the skin. Waiting for the night, he made his getaway.

The letter reached Ezo Chrysanthemum the next day. Although she was sorry for what he had done, it could not be helped now. As there was no question of covering up the letter, she showed it to the Lord Hyobu. Hyobu had a good belly laugh at it. The samurai who happened to be in attendance also had a good laugh. The contrast between Kakita and Sazaé seemed the funniest thing in the world to them. It became an oft-repeated joke. But no one could understand why Sazaé had grown noticeably frail and forlorn-looking.

Sazaé could not at all fathom why Kakita had acted so. But she was a wise young woman. There's something behind this, she thought. Enduring her painful, lonely feelings, she did not speak to anyone about it. When told by Ezo Chrysanthemum to hand over Kakita's letters, she said that she had already burned them. Immediately afterward, she did burn them. And so, the affair between Kakita and Sazaé survived merely as a source of laughter for everybody.

Some time afterwards, Harada Kai came on a visit. He and Hyobu conferred by themselves for a while in the tea arbor of the detached quarters. Then, their business finished, they came back to the banquet hall and commenced a saké carousal with their henchmen. As a likely matter for jest, Hyobu brought up the story of Kakita and Sazaé. At first, Kai laughed along with him. Gradually, though, a strange look came over his face. In the end, he had an expression of extreme displeasure.

Kai told Hyobu to come back with him to the detached quarters. The two had another secret conference. Presently, Ezo Chrysanthemum and Sazaé were summoned. Sazaé was harshly questioned by Kai. There was nothing for it now but to tell the truth, she thought. Unflinchingly, she stated the facts of the case. Kai's face showed more displeasure than ever.

Sazaé was immediately sent back to her parents' house. There, she was kept under surveillance. As for Ezo Chrysanthemum, she requested of her own accord to be relieved of her duties.

Soon after, what is called the Daté Insurrection broke out. As everyone knows, after a long, confused struggle, it ended in the defeat of the Harada Kai faction.

At the close of the rebellion, Kakita resumed his true name. He went in search of Masujiro, who had similarly used an alias, but the latter's whereabouts were completely unknown. Most likely, he had been killed in secret ambush at Kai's behest.

It would be good to be able to tell how the love of Kakita and Sazaé came out in the end, but the things of the past are not to be found out now. The facts are unknown.

✲

✲

Incident on the Afternoon of November Third

✲

A warm south wind, unusual for late autumn, was blowing. It was a day of disagreeable sensations. My head felt strangely heavy, my skin sticky. Sprawled by myself on the tatami in the parlor, I was looking at travel guides. Although I had no immediate travel plans, just the idea of travel seemed cooling on a day like today. If I fell asleep, I thought, I would sleep a while. Just then, my cousin, who lives in Nedo, came to call.

Getting up, I went out onto the veranda. Washing his feet in the overflow of the garden well, my cousin remarked:

"There's been a lot of artillery noise today."

"I heard some over there. From around Koganegahara, most likely."

"Maneuvers have already begun. When I was at the station yesterday, there were a lot of horses."

Wiping his feet, my cousin stepped up onto the veranda. We went into a room where there were chairs. Noticing the guide in my hand, my cousin asked:

"Are you looking at things like that with a getaway in mind?"

We talked about trips. If one was going to Kyushu, an Australia-bound boat was more interesting than the train. We looked up the train and boat fares for Nagasaki.

Four or five bees were dully buzzing around the room. At this time of year, the cold-enfeebled bees always came and clustered on the ceiling of this sunny room. This year, my children might try to grab them, so whenever I saw one I killed it with a flyswatter. Even now, as I chatted with my cousin, I was killing them and tossing them outside. "It's seventy-three degrees today."

"Seventy-three degrees? What do you mean?"

"Seventy-three is hot for this time of year, isn't it? If we were up in the mountains, it would be the height of summer."

"It's muggy, too. No wonder I feel thick in the head like this," my cousin agreed. "I've been napping up to now." Scrunching up his face, he raked the fingers of both hands back through his slightly overgrown crewcut.

"It's been a long time since we took a walk together."

"Let's take one now."

"Shall we go to Shibazaki and buy a wild duck?"

I had my wife bring my purse and a handkerchief.

"What will you do in town? Can we have the duck for supper tonight?"

"No, not tonight."

My cousin and I went out through the garden onto the mountainside in back. To the north, the sky was clouding over somewhat menacingly. Emerging from the fields onto the Ne no Kami road, we went on a ways, turning off through the fields again toward the grade school. In the distance, a detachment of cavalry appeared, crossing the Narita line intersection. They all had scraps of white cloth wound around their caps.

A while later, we crossed the intersection ourselves. A company of cavalry approached, this time from behind us. They were still fairly far away. Not paying them much attention, we went along talking. But with a rather startling rapidity, they were soon right in back of us.

"Pursuing the enemy, I suppose," my cousin said.

Despite the muggy heat, all of the men were wearing greatcoats. Probably they'd been told not to take them off no matter how hot it got. Only their caps they all carried in their hands. Around these, too, scraps of white cloth had been wound. Even so, when the young officer at their head half turned and gave a brief command, they put them back on. Beads of sweat trickled down their faces, as if they had come out of a steam bath. Without a word, they hurried on past us, accompanied by the strange unpleasant smell of leather and perspiration.

About seventy-five feet in length, the file quickly went by. Observing one man lagging behind exhausted, my cousin said:

"A lot of their gear doesn't fit their bodies. You'd think the army would make it better."

"Does that man have two greatcoats?"

"You mean that roll attached to his knapsack? That's a bedroll, more likely."

The soldiers receded into the distance. On the road, fresh unaccustomed horse manure was scattered about in abundance. Walking along, my cousin and I chatted about the marches we'd gone on in our middle school days.

From the intersection of the Tokiwa line, we'd come up the gradual slope of the railway cut a short ways when in the mulberry fields beyond we saw a skirmish taking place. Groups of farmers, here and there, were looking on.

Turning off the main road, we took a palisaded shortcut to a temple called Togen-ji, famous for its *kaya* trees. To our left, on a road through the fields, seven or eight cavalrymen were letting their horses saunter at leisure. A few minutes later, descending a narrow sloping path through a bamboo grove, we arrived at the poultry shop.

There was not a single wild duck to be had, the man said. He'd sent every last one to Tokyo that morning. "What I have here now are mandarin ducks," he added. We had a look at them. Not the least bit tame as yet, huddled in a corner of the pen, only looking at us out of one eye, they seemed very much afraid of us. "The male is still a duckling. They were caught separately, so they're not parent and child. He's been squashed by the female," the man said by way of explanation. The male, his stomach pressed to the ground, could only waddle around on his backside.

There had to be wild ducks somewhere in the neighborhood, so I told the man to go get me one. While he was gone, my cousin and I strolled to the Toné embankment, about a hundred and twenty yards farther on. Although I say "embankment," the present course of the river was two and a half miles away. Between lay a broad marsh, where stands of water oats flourished densely.

Two or three shots rang out in rapid fire. Nearby, a wild duck gave a flustered squawk. In the distance, a flock of young ducks flew up. The shooting continued. Panicked, the flock whirled up slowly into the sky.

Along the embankment, twenty cavalrymen or so came galloping toward us. The shooting stopped. Descending the embankment, we went back the way we had come.

Ahead, at the crossroads, an officer with a map in his hand and two or three of his men were making loud inquiries. From the far side of a paddy, the poultryman's old wife was yelling back at them. The officer and his men hurried off in the direction they'd been given.

Reaching the crossroads ourselves, we met up with the poultryman. In his hand, a blue-headed wild duck dangled by its pinioned wings. At the sight of its head innocently sticking out, the idea of its being killed in a few minutes was hateful. To come out to buy a bird for the pot and to go back with a not very appealing wild duck as a pet needed thinking about. Nevertheless, I decided to take it home.

When we got to the shop, the poultryman went along the dirt-floored passage and out back with the duck. It struck me that he was about to kill it. In a vague way, I decided it was no great matter if he did. But then my cousin said:

"Hasn't he gone to kill it?" Then I called out:

"Hey. Don't kill that duck."

"You'll take it like this?"

The poultryman, his hands still set to wring the duck's neck, came back into the entryway.

The wild duck neither struggled nor cried out. Having it wrapped in a carrying-cloth, we left the shop.

When we'd come as far back as the palisaded shortcut to Togen-ji, we saw two or three cavalry horses tied up at a farmer's house nearby.

"The soldiers are lying down. I wonder what's happened," my cousin said, peering in at the farmer's house. If you kept moving, you could see inside fleetingly through the gaps in the hedge. "Maybe they're resting. Their hats don't have any scraps of cloth. The enemy must have gotten away."

As we came out onto the main road, we saw a soldier, stripped to the waist, lying face up on his knapsack by the roadside. Another soldier was nursing him. Spreading a handkerchief on his chest, he dripped some water onto it from his canteen. The fallen man, his eyes closed, his mouth slackly open, did not seem to be clear in his head. Only his face, covered with sweat, was rather flushed. It gave me a queer feeling. I didn't want to stop and look.

A while later, when we'd come down the gentle slope of the railway cut, we encountered a company of infantry. About two hundred strong, they were marching at a fairly rapid clip. About halfway along the file, I saw another soldier who was at the end of his strength. A mate on either side wedging an arm under his shoulder, he staggered forward at the same quickstep pace of the others. His eyes were no longer open. As if in a drunken stupor, his head snapped back at each step, unable to hold itself up, or wagged left and right.

Another man like him went by. On his face, there was no expression whatsoever. I had the feeling that he was in such pain that there was no longer any expression of pain. As he crossed the intersection, his foot caught against one of the tracks. He pitched forward as if he'd been booted from behind. His comrades were too weak to hold him up. The fallen man said nothing. He just lay there.

The quickstepping soldiers, delayed for a moment, piled up one after the other in back of him.

"Don't stop!" their officer yelled. Like a stream divided by a rock, the men split into two files and passed on by. Although eyeing the fallen man, none of them said a word. All of them, eyeing him, silently hurried past.

"Hey! Get up! Aren't going to get up, eh?" Standing by his head, a corporal shouted at the man. One of the soldiers, taking the man by his arm, tried to pull him to his feet. The corporal kept on shouting. The fallen man tried to get up. Contracting his body from his sprawled out position, he got his hips up a little. But there was no strength left in him. He collapsed weakly. He tried again, two or three times. It was like the sort of thing I'd seen in plays, when one of the characters had received his death-blow. The memory came back to me with a certain displeasure. The fallen man was a one-year volunteer. Compared to his fellows, he was short and frail-looking.

"This is no good. Take his things off him," the corporal commanded. The wife of the railway watchman, ladling water into a hand-bucket, hurried up. I could not look at any more of this. A feeling akin to fury rose up in me. Then the tears came.

My cousin, who had caught up with me, said:

"Their officer kept saying they couldn't rest, they couldn't rest."

Less than forty feet farther on, another man was down. Although his strength was gone, this soldier, naked to the waist, his eyes half shut, struggled to his feet and tried to march. He, too, did not utter a word.

"It's all right. You don't have to get up," said the soldier nursing him, holding him back. In the rice paddy below the road, another soldier was dipping his canteen into the water. A strange look on his face, my cousin pointed him out.

Another sixty feet along, another man had fallen. Each of these men had only a vague absence of expression.

We met a young, slightly built soldier, two knapsacks piled atop his own, a rifle slung over each shoulder, silently marching on alone.

A little ways on, there was another man down.

"May I have some water?" Raising his eyes, the soldier nursing him called out to four soldiers passing by. "Neither of us has a drop."

"I have some, I think." Halting, one of the men took out his canteen and handed it to the soldier.

The soldier fed a trickle of water into the mouth of his comrade, who lay face up with his eyes closed. Then, after he'd sprinkled a few drops on his forehead, two or three on the handkerchief spread out on his chest, as if in some kind of ritual, so as not to use up the meager supply, he thanked the soldier and handed back the canteen. The soldier hurried off after his mates.

After this, along a stretch of about three hundred yards, we saw four or five more such men.

In front of the grade school, my cousin and I split up and went our ways. Hurrying back along the road through the evening fields by myself, I grew excited again. The matter was excessively obvious, I thought. It was the sort of thing that sooner or later would be absolutely clear to anyone. Any way one looked at it, it was excessively obvious. The whole thing was due to ignorance.

At some point, I lost my way. I didn't turn off where I should have done. Having gone all the way to the Ne no Kami road, I had to backtrack.

As soon as I got home, I took the wild duck out of the furoshiki for a look. Its head was wedged face up beneath its crosswise pinioned wings. I released it in the shack where until recently I'd raised pigeons. But the wild duck was half dead. Beating its wings, it tried to run along the ground, but it couldn't lift up its head. Stretching out its neck, it merely rubbed it against the ground as it pushed itself forward. Taking it outside, I tried letting it go in the pond. But somehow it couldn't float right. Immediately flipping over, its white belly showing, it flapped and floundered about futilely. I felt intensely annoyed.

"Oh, look. Daddy has bought a wild duck." My wife had come outside with our baby daughter in her arms.

"It's not something to look at. Go away," I said, in an unaccountably foul humor. Calling the maid, I told her to take the wild duck to the farmer's next door to be killed. I no longer wanted my family to have it. The next day, I sent it to friends.

✲

✲

The Shopboy's God

✲

Senkichi was an apprentice at a scales shop in Kanda.

The autumnal, mild, clear sunlight, underneath the faded blue shop curtain, quietly shone into the shop. There were no customers. The senior clerk, sitting behind the latticework of the counter, was languidly smoking a cigarette. He began to talk to the junior clerk who was reading a newspaper by the brazier.

"Ko-san. Won't be long now. You'll be able to have some of that fat tuna you like."

"Yeah."

"How about it? Shall we go this evening, after closing shop?"

"Fine with me."

"It's only fifteen minutes by the Outer Moat trolley."

"That's right."

"Reason I mention it is, you can't eat the stuff around here."

"That's for sure."

The shopboy Senkichi sat respectfully in his place, a short distance from the junior clerk, his hands under his apron. "Ah, they're talking about sushi," he thought as he listened. There was a branch shop in Kyobashi. Now and then he was sent there on an errand, so that he knew precisely where that sushi shop was. How he longed to become a clerk soon! Then, making that kind of knowledgeable remark, he could step inside such a shop any time he liked!

"By the way, Yohei's son has opened a shop near the Matsuya. Did you know that, Ko-san?"

"No, I didn't. Where's the Matsuya?"

"I'm not sure myself, but I think it's the one near the new bridge."

"Oh? Is the sushi good there?"

"So they say."

"What's it called? 'Yohei's' too?"

"Uh, what was it, now? Something. I heard the name, but I've forgotten."

Senkichi, listening, thought: So there are shops as famous as that. Then, he thought: But when they say "good," just how do they mean "good"? Carefully, so as not to make any noise, he swallowed the saliva that had gathered in his mouth.

Two or three evenings after this, Senkichi was sent on an errand to the Kyobashi shop. As he'd set out, he'd been handed his round-trip trolley fare by the clerk.

Getting off the Outer Moat trolley at Kajibashi, Senkichi purposely passed in front of the sushi shop. Gazing up at the shop curtain, he imagined all the clerks briskly parting the sections of the curtain as they went inside. He was feeling pretty hungry just then. He pictured to himself the fatty, yellow-tinged tuna sushi. What he would do for one piece, he thought. Often, when he'd been given a round-trip fare, he had bought a one-way ticket and walked back. Now, also, the leftover four sen chinked in his inside chest pocket. With four sen, I could have one, he thought. But you can't say "I'll have just one, please." Giving up the idea, he went on by the shop.

His business at the scales shop was soon done. Carrying a small cardboard carton, surprisingly heavy with its numerous little brass weights, he left the shop.

Feeling somehow led on, he went back the way he had come. About to turn off toward the sushi shop, he happened to spot another stall, up an alley across from the intersection, with the same name on its curtain. Idly, he bent his steps toward it.

Awano, the young member of the House of Peers, had been told by his fellow member Banda that the pleasure of sushi could not be understood unless you ate it with your fingers straight from the hands that shaped it. Sometime, he thought, he'd like to try that sort of stand-up sushi snack. He'd had his friend give him the name of a good sushi stall.

One day, just before sunset, crossing the Kyobashi Bridge from the Ginza, Awano went to that sushi stall he'd been told about. Three or four customers were ahead of him. Hesitating a moment, he made up his mind and went inside. For a while, not wanting to force himself in among the others, he stood in back, just inside the shop curtain.

Suddenly, a shopboy of twelve or thirteen entered. Brushing past Awano, he stood in a small space in front of the latter and busily eyed the slanted counter board of thick Zelkova wood where five or six pieces of sushi were displayed.

"Don't you have just rice wrapped in seaweed?"

"Aah, not today." The corpulent proprietor, molding a piece of sushi, stared questioningly at the boy.

With a determined air, as if to show this wasn't his first time, the shopboy abruptly put out his hand and took one of the three or so pieces of tuna sushi lined up on the board. Strangely, though, having shot his hand out with such alacrity, he was very hesitant as he drew it back.

"One piece is six sen, you know," the proprietor said.

Silently, as if dropping it, the shopboy put the sushi back.

"You can't leave it there after you've touched it." Replacing it with the piece he'd just made, the proprietor took it off the counter.

The shopboy didn't say a word. Making a face, he stood glued to the spot. Then, quickly summoning a kind of courage, he went out under the shop curtain.

"Nowadays even sushi has gone up. It's not something for shopboys," the proprietor said, looking slightly uncomfortable. Then, after finishing another piece, he deftly tossed the one the shopboy had touched into his mouth and wolfed it.

"The other day, I went to that sushi stall you told me about."

"How was it?"

"Not bad. I noticed that everybody held it this way, the fish side down. Is that the way to do it?"

"Yes. With tuna, that's the way it's done."

"Why do they hold it fish side down?"

"So when the fish is bad, you'll know it right away by the hot taste on your tongue."

"You sound like a pretty fishy connoisseur," laughed Awano.

Then, Awano told his friend about the shopboy.

"I felt sorry for him, somehow. I wanted to do something for him," he said.

"Why didn't you treat him? I bet he would have been overjoyed if you'd said he could have as many as he could eat."

"He would have been overjoyed, but I would have been in a cold sweat."

"A cold sweat? You mean you don't have the courage for it?"

"I don't know if it's courage or not, but I just couldn't have done it. Maybe if we had gone out together, and I'd treated him somewhere else, but . . ."

"Yes, it's that kind of thing," Banda agreed.

Awano, thinking he would like to measure by weight the gradual growth of his little boy who was in kindergarten, decided to install a small scales in his bathroom. One day, he happened to pass Senkichi's shop in Kanda.

Senkichi did not know who Awano was. But Awano recognized Senkichi.

On the concrete pavement that led to the back of the shop, seven or eight freight scales, ranging from small to large, were lined up in a neat row. Awano selected the smallest one. A replica of the ones you saw in railway stations and shipping offices, the pretty miniature would probably delight his wife and boy, Awano thought.

The clerk, taking out an old-fashioned account book, asked:

"What is the address, sir?"

"Well . . ." Awano, looking at Senkichi, thought a moment. "Is that boy free just now?"

"Yes. He's not particularly busy . . ."

"If that's so, may I have him come with me? I'm in a bit of a hurry."

"Certainly, sir. I'll have him put it in a cart and accompany you immediately."

In compensation for not having treated the boy the other day, Awano thought, he would do it for him somewhere today.

"Now, if you'll write your name and address here, sir." After Awano had paid, the clerk brought out another account book.

Awano was somewhat flustered. He didn't know that when one buys a scales the number of the scales has to be registered along with the name and address of the buyer. Awano had the feeling that if he treated the boy after having given his name, he would get into a muck of cold sweat. After long thought, he wrote down a made-up name and address and handed the book back to the clerk.

Taking his time, the customer strolled on ahead. Senkichi, pulling the little cart loaded with the scales, stayed about fifteen feet behind him.

When they came to a rickshaw stand, the customer, having Senkichi wait, went inside. A few minutes later, the scales were transferred to one of the rickshaws.

"Take care of it. You'll be paid at the destination. That's on the card too." Having given these instructions, the customer emerged from the stand. Then, to Senkichi, he said with a smile: "You've worked hard. I want to buy you a little something. Let's walk over there."

Senkichi felt this was both too good to be true and a little scary. He was happy nonetheless. He quickly bobbed his head two or three times in thanks.

They went by a noodle shop, a sushi shop, and a fried chicken shop. "Where does he want to go?" Senkichi began to feel a trifle uneasy. Passing underneath the elevated tracks of Kanda Station, they went by the Matsuya. Crossing the trolley tracks, they came to a small sushi stall up an alley. Here the customer stopped.

"Wait here a moment." Saying this to Senkichi, the customer went inside. Senkichi, letting down the shafts of the cart, stood quietly.

Soon the customer came out. Behind him was the young, refined-looking proprietress, who said to Senkichi:

"Shopboy. Please come in."

"I'm going back now, so have enough to eat." Saying this, the customer, as if he were running away, hurried off in the direction of the trolley line.

Instantly gobbling them down like a skinny, starved dog that has come upon unexpected food, Senkichi had three adult-sized pieces of sushi. There were no other customers. Sliding the door shut, the proprietress purposely withdrew. Without worrying about how he looked, Senkichi was able to gorge himself to his heart's content.

When she came out to pour him a cup of tea, the proprietress asked:

"Won't you have something more?"

Senkichi blushed. "No, I've had plenty." He hung his head. Then, busily, he got ready to leave.

"Well, come again, then. There's still lots of money left over."

Senkichi was silent.

"Did you know that gentleman from before?"

"No."

"Wha-at?" The proprietress exchanged glances with her husband, who had just come out.

"He's a very fashionable gentleman. But unless you come back, shopboy, we won't know what to do with the rest of the money."

Senkichi, slipping into his clogs, could only bow frantically.

Awano, after he'd left the shopboy and, with a feeling of being pursued, had come to the trolley line, hailed a passing cab and went straight to Banda's house.

He had a strangely lonely feeling. The other day, seeing the crestfallen look of that shopboy, he'd truly felt sorry for him. Today, by a chance opportunity, he'd been able to do what he'd thought he would like to do if possible. The shopboy must be contented, and he should be contented. It was not a bad thing to make another person happy. It was only natural if he himself felt a certain happiness. Then why was there this strangely lonely, unpleasant feeling? Where did it come from? It was like the feeling one has after having done something bad in secret.

Perhaps, from the self-consciousness of having performed a good deed, it was criticized, mocked, betrayed by his true feelings, and was felt as this kind of lonely emotion. Perhaps if he thought of it in a slightly more modest, casual way, it would be all right. Without meaning to, he'd made a thing of it. But, after all, it was not as if he'd done something shameful. At least, it wasn't something that should leave this bad feeling behind, he thought.

He had promised to call that day, so Banda was expecting him. In the evening, they went in Banda's car to a concert.

Awano got home late that night. His strange, lonely feeling, after an evening with his friend and the spirited solos of the lady singer, was almost completely gone.

"Thank you very much for the scales." As he'd expected, his wife had been delighted with the little scales. The boy was asleep, but he'd been very happy too, she said.

"By the way, that shopboy I saw the other day at the sushi stall? I met him again."

"Oh? Where?"

"He's the apprentice at the scales shop."

"My, what a coincidence."

Awano told his wife how he'd treated the shopboy to sushi, and of his lonely feeling afterward.

"Why was that, I wonder? A lonely feeling like that. It's strange." His good-hearted wife knit her brows, thinking. Then, suddenly, she said: "Yes. I know that feeling."

"That kind of thing happens," she went on. "Whatever it was, it was that kind of thing."

"Do you think so?"

"Yes, truly, it's that kind of thing. What did Banda say?"

"I didn't tell him about it."

"Oh. Still, the shopboy must have been very happy. Anybody would be at that sort of unexpected treat. I'd like one myself. Won't you order me some of that sushi on the telephone?"

Senkichi, pulling the empty cart, went on his way. He was gorged with sushi. Often before he had eaten his fill. But he could not remember ever having filled himself with such delicious food.

Suddenly, he remembered his humiliating experience at the sushi stall in Kyobashi the other day. It finally came back to him. Only now, he realized that in some way it was connected with today's feast. Maybe that man had been there, he thought. He must have been. But how had he known where Senkichi worked? This was a little strange. Come to think of it, the place he'd been taken to today was the same place the clerks had talked about that time. How did that customer come to know even about their idle talk?

It was a great mystery. Senkichi was unable to guess that Awano and Banda, just like the clerks, had had a sushi shop chat themselves. He could only think that the customer, simultaneously knowing about the clerks' conversation even as Senkichi had been listening to it, had therefore taken him to the place today. If that were not so, he thought, why had he passed by the two or three sushi shops before it?

At any rate, the customer began to seem like no ordinary personage. Knowing about Senkichi's humiliation, about the clerks' conversation, and above all knowing the thoughts of Senkichi's heart, he had bestowed that ample treat. This was not the act of a human being. Perhaps he was a god. Or, if not that, a wizard. Perhaps he was the fox god.

The reason Senkichi thought of the fox god was because he had an aunt who every now and then was possessed by this god. When the fox god moved into her, she would shake and shudder, make weird prophecies and accurately describe events in faraway places. Senkichi had seen her once when she was that way. It seemed a trifle odd that the fox god should be such a stylish gentleman. Nevertheless, his feeling that the gentleman was a supernatural being kept on getting stronger.

In time, Awano's strange, lonely feeling vanished without a trace. But he felt a queer twinge of conscience whenever he passed the Kanda shop, and in the end he became unable to do so. He also became unwilling to go to that sushi stall by himself.

"It doesn't matter," his wife laughed. "Order some by telephone. Then we'll all be able to have a treat."

Awano, unsmilingly, said: "That's not the sort of thing a timid person like myself finds so easy to do."

For Senkichi, "that customer" became an ever more unforgettable figure. By now, it hardly mattered whether he was a human being or a supernatural being. There was only this great thankfulness. Although he'd been asked back two or three times by the proprietor and his wife, he felt no desire to regale himself again. The idea of taking such advantage frightened him.

Always, at lonely or difficult times, he thought of "that customer." Just thinking about him became a sort of consolation. Senkichi believed that some day "that customer" would come to him again, bringing an unexpected blessing.

Here the writer lays down his pen. Actually, he'd thought of ending the story this way: the shopboy, wanting to know the true identity of "that customer," learns his name and address from the clerk and goes looking for the place. Instead of a house at that address, he finds a little shrine to the fox god. The shopboy is astonished. But the writer came to feel that such an ending would be somewhat cruel to the shopboy. And so he decided to lay down his pen at the aforesaid place.

✲

✲

Rain Frogs

✲

Eight miles to the north of ———, there is a small village called ———. A long, narrow hamlet strung out along one road, it has many hedges and few shops. The inhabitants, mostly old indigenous stock, had split up and multiplied in branch families, so that the more than a hundred households shared but five or six surnames. Accustomed to saying "so-and-so at the corner," "so-and-so in front of the bamboo grove," or "so-and-so at the pole shop," even now, when the bamboo grove had been down for ten years and "so-and-so" had given up the pole shop a generation ago, people still made use of such terms to distinguish persons of the same surname.

There had always been a cooperative in the hamlet, by which folks helped each other. By now, there were many who did not even know who had founded it. The road running through the hamlet was better than the prefectural roads. But the lanes that entered it from either side, muddy quagmires in the winter thaws and rainy season, were but lines of flat stones wide enough for one person.

For instance, when a house burnt down, for it to be rebuilt just as it had been cost not even half what it normally would. The lumber came free of charge from the communal forest on the mountain, and the labor was donated by so many persons per household.

But even in a place like this, there were sometimes those who were not content with country life. Going up to the city, they would take a job, not do well at it and come back. Even then, the villagers did not grudge them enough help to keep their families together. If they gained the cooperative's approval, they could borrow money at low interest. It was that sort of village.

In the heart of the village, there was a saké brewery, built in the storehouse style, run by a family named Minoya. Sanjiro, its young proprietor, was an only child. By his father's wish, he had attended agricultural college in his middle school days, and was expected to carry on the family business afterward. Five or six years ago, however, the father had died. Sanjiro abruptly found himself the young master of the household.

There having been a single head clerk ever since the days of Sanjiro's grandfather, the business continued to run smoothly. The grandmother maintaining that the master should be in the house, however, Sanjiro had been called back from his dormitory in the city and installed. He had no objections to that, though. He hadn't had any dreams of becoming a doctor of agricultural science so as to give the people of the region a better saké. Besides, he felt relieved simply to not have them say that he gave himself airs as a university man.

He had a close friend called Takeno Shigeo. After graduating from middle school, Takeno had studied literature at a private university in Tokyo, publishing his poems and songs in literary magazines under the pen name Green Leaf. Well up on the doings of the literary world, he often talked to Sanjiro about them.

But Sanjiro had no thoughts of writing himself. He didn't think he could, for one thing, and for another felt no interest in trying. He didn't even read that much. So he hadn't paid much attention to Takeno's anecdotes. After his return to the village, though, when life there had begun to seem a shade monotonous, his friend's influence surfaced in him. Each time he went to the city, he came back with some book or other.

Takeno, meanwhile, commencing a correspondence with a

fellow contributor, had not long after advanced to marriage talks with the lady. The daughter of a Tokyo fruiterer, she was not beautiful but she was strong-minded for her age.

A third son, Takeno had thought himself free to marry as he wished. But his considerably older brother, the first son, had unexpectedly opposed the match. To start with, he didn't care for the fact that the girl was a writer. The parents, having retired from family affairs, left everything up to him, so that his disapproval was the same as the family's disapproval. Takeno, angered, cut off relations with them. He made up his mind to support himself by opening a fruit shop with the girl in a nearby town.

At this time, Sanjiro of the Minoya also got married, to a farm girl whose family was distantly related to his own. Having always liked the girl, he'd gone along willingly with his grandmother's suggestion.

The girl's name was Seki. Taciturn and none too quick, she had no education. But she was a true country beauty. Although she was bothered by her short stature, her beautifully proportioned arms and legs kept it from being uncomely. Her head was small, with a wealth of thick hair that had a reddish tinge. But the smoothness of her skin, the regular shape of her nose and a feeling of firm elasticity about her whole body made her seem healthy just to look at and gave pleasure to all who saw her. If there was one defect of which she was unaware, it was that there was no light in her tea-brown eyes.

Before long, Seki was pregnant. In her fifth month, toward the end of autumn, she came down with the then prevalent influenza. The family worried about this illness during pregnancy, and sure enough she suffered a miscarriage. Although Seki herself soon recovered, her mother-in-law, who'd worried the most about her, ended by contracting the same illness. This developed into pneumonia, and she eventually died of it.

That had been three years ago. Seki did not become pregnant again. The impatient grandmother often brought up the subject, causing a bitter look to come into Sanjiro's face. But Seki herself paid her no mind.

After the faithful old clerk Okakura had fallen prey to palsy and retired to his home town, Sanjiro, left on his own, had to do everything in the family business. So it appeared—actually, however, the doughty grandmother, from long experience, managed all matters in his behalf.

Bit by bit, Sanjiro's interest in literature had grown. Placing a large bookcase in the parlor, he enjoyed the gradual accumulation of new publications there. Lately, he'd taken to writing short pieces and showing them to Takeno.

He thought of trying to impart a taste for such things to Seki. By himself, it was somehow lonely. But that was too much to expect of Seki. Remembering his own backwardness, he could imagine how it would be for her. Therefore he was neither disappointed nor resigned.

One day a postcard came from Takeno. The playwright S and the novelist G would be speaking at the town hall in a few days, and he was by all means to come. Sanjiro thought he would take Seki along. Saying so in his reply, he added that perhaps Takeno could put them up for the night.

The day came. Although it was fine weather for October, a disagreeably warm wind was blowing. As the lectures began at three, Sanjiro decided to set out for town after an early lunch. During the preparations, his grandmother, who'd been assisting in them, abruptly collapsed. It was nothing serious, but her spirits were low and leaving her in the care of the servants was out of the question. Sanjiro said to Seki:

"What shall we do? Takeno is expecting us. How would it be if you went by yourself? If you go, I'll be able to hear about the lectures from you. Won't you go?"

"Yes."

"There's nothing to worry about if I stay with Grandmother. You go and have a good time."

"Yes," replied Seki, turning her innocent eyes on him.

Soon, ensconced in the rickshaw that had been waiting outside, Seki set off. Standing in front of the shop, Sanjiro watched the rickshaw go off into the distance. Her low pompadour (done in the "eaves" style which nowadays one did not see much even in the country) all atremble in the vehicle's vibrations, not once turning around, Seki slowly receded down the long, straight, hedge-lined road.

His grandmother had a slight fever, and her face was unusually flushed. Reading a book by the bedside of the dozing invalid, Sanjiro now and then wrung out and changed the cold cloths for her forehead.

Outside the saké storehouse, workmen were tightening the hoops of a big cask. The dry sound of their mallets, mingling with the wind, could be heard in the sickroom. Now and then, Sanjiro stepped out to see how the job was going.

What was she doing, about now? At odd moments, Sanjiro thought of Seki. As he imagined her solitary figure, engulfed in the overflow audience, it only then dawned upon him that she would be completely out of place in such a scene.

That evening, laying out his bedding alongside his grandmother's, he retired early. How long had it been, he thought, since he had slept in the same room with his grandmother?

At nightfall, the wind had died down. But now there was the sporadic sound of raindrops on the eaves. It was a curiously sultry night. Sanjiro found it difficult to sleep. The sick person's fever seemed to have abated somewhat, and she was fast asleep, breathing calmly. The rain gradually increased in intensity.

The next morning, when Sanjiro got up, the sky was beautifully clear. The wind had veered to the north, and there was a bracing autumnal crispness in the air. It was a morning that made one feel good. His grandmother, who had risen earlier, her gray hair bound neatly in a bun, was already busy in the kitchen.

"There are some things I have to buy. I thought I'd go into town and meet Seki. Are you well again?"

"Yes, I'm all better now."

After breakfast, Sanjiro decided to set out for town immediately. It having suddenly turned cool, he wrapped a shawl for Seki in a bundle kerchief. Fastening it to the handlebars of his bicycle, he set out.

Truly it was a morning that made one feel good to be alive. The fine gravel of the roadway had been rinsed fresh and clean, and dewdrops glittered like jewels on the trees and grasses. In the fields, against the wet, black earth, the purple flowers of the scallions seemed extraordinarily beautiful. In the distant sky, a faint line of geese winged its way. Feeling a carefree pleasure, Sanjiro sped along on his bicycle.

When he dismounted outside Takeno's fruit shop, the latter was prying open on a ditch-board a crate of apples that apparently had come a long ways. As he raised his face, until then lowered and red with effort, a look of consternation floated across it. Seki, he told Sanjiro, had spent the night at the Cloud-Viewing Pavilion. She was not here now. Sanjiro's eyes grew wide. At first, the contrast of Seki and the Cloud-Viewing Pavilion seemed excessively comical. As the most elegant and expensive inn of the town, the Cloud-Viewing Pavilion was thought of as off-bounds to people like themselves. But Sanjiro's amusement was quickly converted to unease by a certain significant air of Takeno's.

Discarding his work apron on the spot, Takeno led Sanjiro inside. From the head of the dusky ladder-stairs, he showed him into a room on the low-ceilinged second floor of the shop. There, he gave Sanjiro the details of what had happened.

The day before, it had been evening by the time the lectures ended. Afterward, there was a reception sponsored by the town newspaper at a teahouse-restaurant called Pure Gardens, the mansion of a feudal lord in the old days. Takeno had attended. Seki and his wife, however, having been introduced that afternoon in the green room by a local music teacher called Yamazaki Yoshié, had promised to meet S and G after the party at the

Cloud-Viewing Pavilion. With Yoshié, they waited for them there.

By the time S and G, sent off in an automobile in the heavy rain, finally arrived, it was after ten o'clock. Both men were more or less drunk. But at first, at least, they were comparatively well-behaved.

S, a fair-complexioned man, had gentle eyes and a broad forehead hidden slantwise by his soft hair. Polite in his manner of speech, with a low voice, he was a man whose very gestures somehow gave an impression of the feminine. G, on the other hand, a man whose eyes, nose, chin, and neck were all strongly drawn, a broad-shouldered, powerfully built man, gave off a feeling of might. To Takeno's wife, that impression of strength was somehow frightening.

Fruit and sweet saké were brought in for the ladies. Seki and Takeno's wife did not have much of either. Only Yoshié, downing one drink after another, had a good time by herself.

Yoshie's relationships with men were a source of much gossip. Her liaison with S, also, to those in the know, was something of an open secret. Although the rumors about her were not too savory, with her opulent physique, sexy voice, and flashy personality she was considered indispensable by the town's young set.

There was a lot of lighthearted chatter. The conversation of the two men was more interesting than their lectures had been. G, in particular, talked about whatever he felt like. Skillfully concealing their crudity, he ended up talking about things that were not usually brought up in the presence of ladies.

Seki, completely overawed, an empty smile on her face, looked at the others with lonely eyes. Takeno's wife felt sorry for her, but there was no sign of the rain's letting up. When, finally, she made preparations for leaving, Yoshié, who was rather deep in her cups, strenuously detained her. Thinking it better to leave her on her own, Takeno's wife lightly parried her. But Yoshié, carried along by her own momentum, insisted more and more stubbornly. Since Yoshié was the kind who had to have their own way even if they didn't care one way or another, Takeno's wife made ready to leave nonetheless. In the end, Yoshié grew truly angry. "If that's so, then I'll leave with you," she said recklessly, looking as if about to cry and with a sidelong glance at the men. In a wheedling tone, she added: "That's right, G. I'm going with them."

"Is that so?" G replied, with deliberate indifference. "But doesn't S have some business with you?"

"No jokes allowed." S was grinning broadly.

"Well, how about Yoshié? Doesn't she have some business with you?"

Yoshié, getting to her feet with brusque alacrity, went over to G and thumped him twice on the back. G assumed an impassive expression. Takeno's wife felt that she could not stay any longer. With the astonished Seki in tow, she started to leave. Yoshié came over with a grim look in her eyes.

"If that's how you want it, I won't keep you. I'll just keep Seki-san. It's all the same where Seki-san stays for the night, isn't it? It's out of the question for her to go back in this downpour."

"If it's all right, why doesn't she stay here for the night?" S chimed in.

"Yes." Smiling docilely, Seki gave a slight nod of assent.

"You will stay, then?"

"Any place is fine."

Takeno's wife was taken aback. Before she knew what to say, she was pushed out into the corridor by the powerful Yoshié. S got up and came out to see her off. Behind him, Yoshié called after her triumphantly:

"No matter who you are, you can't be a stuck-up prude all the time!"

Sanjiro could not understand the purport of this story. It seemed a matter of no importance, yet it also seemed somehow a terribly troubling event. He could not make out which. But the tense solemnity with which Takeno told the story was out of the ordinary.

Below, a rickshaw stopped. Takeno hurried downstairs. Shortly afterward his angry voice was heard, upbraiding his wife.

"She's come back with an outlandish hairdo." Looking disgusted, Takeno came back upstairs.

"What kind of hairdo?"

"I'll soon make her change it."

"It doesn't matter, does it? I'd like to see it myself. Her other one was too old-fashioned. She needed something a little more up-to-date." Speaking with intentional cheerfulness, Sanjiro got to his feet and went downstairs. At the foot of the dusky stairs, Seki and Takeno's wife stood vaguely facing each other.

"Let me see your hair." Sanjiro led Seki into the bright part of the shop. The ear-covering hairdo, in the fashionable style called *mimi kakushi*, accompanied by rouged cheeks, became Seki unexpectedly and extraordinarily well.

"Very nice. Very nice." Squeezing his wife's pointed little chin between his fingertips as she kept her eyes shamefacedly lowered, Sanjiro turned her toward him. He actually did not receive the slightest disagreeable feeling from the hairdo. Seki twisted her chin out of his fingers and lowered her eyes again.

"You look tired. Shall we go home now?"

Seki nodded.

"Did you understand the lectures?"

Seki shook her head.

"That's too bad. But I'm told there were songs by Miss Yamazaki. Did she have a good voice?"

Seki nodded.

"Did you and Miss Yamazaki stay at the Cloud-Viewing Pavilion last night?"

Seki shook her head.

"You were left there by yourself?"

Just then, still looking aside, Seki gave a smile whose meaning he could not tell. It startled him. Unthinkingly, he stared at Seki's face. But with a weak, hooded gaze she looked vaguely away, out at the street. After that, Sanjiro did not have the heart to ask her anything more. It seemed like something forbidden, and he himself felt frightened to ask. He was frightened just by Seki, who would give him a straight answer as soon as he did ask.

His feelings were violently roiled.

Deciding to return at once, he went back up the ladder-stairs. At the top, Takeno and his wife were whispering about something. When she heard Sanjiro, the wife hurriedly got to her feet. Waiting for him to come all the way up, she went back downstairs. Sanjiro resolved to act as calmly as he could.

Until the rickshaw came, the two men sat facing each other. But not a word passed between them. Hunched over at the Sentoku copper brazier in which there was no fire, both hands held out, Sanjiro struggled with the void in his heart. Through the slender, vertical apertures of the latticed bay window, the second story of the auctioneer's shop could be seen across the street. Bathed in the soft beams of the autumnal sun, with *Knitted Goods* dyed in white on a red background, its large banner waved back and forth in slow billowings.

"Ah, yes. I brought along a shawl." Just then, Sanjiro remembered that kind of thing.

"The rickshaw has come." Hearing his wife's voice below, Takeno went downstairs. Sanjiro, first looking around the room, not for anything in particular but just in case he'd forgotten something, carefully descended the steep, dusky stairs.

Seki was standing among the produce displays of apples, grapes and bananas and the like. Takeno, his arms folded and with an ill-humored expression, stood in the doorway. Bending over, Sanjiro put on his clogs. Takeno's wife, selecting several apples from the wood shavings of the crate, placed them in a roughwork basket and handed it to the rickshaw man.

"Be sure and come again soon."

"Thank you." Sanjiro, tucking up his kimono from behind, answered in a flat voice.

Although it hadn't been so bad that morning, when the wind blew against you now it was cold. Seki said nothing. Even when

Sanjiro spoke to her, she kept her cheeks buried in the shawl and didn't answer. His sulky, silent wife beside him, with a sense of crushed loneliness and a dread of touching the quick no matter what he said, Sanjiro thought: That's how she is. Earlier, the stylish ear-covering hairdo and rouged cheeks had been pretty, but here on the sunlit country road they were ugly.

Sanjiro didn't feel like saying much himself, but the rickshawman kept up a stream of talk. What kind of thing was post-office insurance, a factory was going up on the edge of town and so dry fields would be more valuable than paddies, the son of so-and-so in Sanjiro's village had graduated from medical school in Niigata and was either coming to the town hospital or setting up practice in the village—the list of such topics was inexhaustible. It became painful for Sanjiro to talk to him. Although worried about her fatigue, he said to Seki: "How about it? Shall we walk the rest of the way?"

When the road to the village branched off from the prefectural road, there was a tall hackberry tree. Smitten by last night's rain, dead leaves lay scattered all about. Seki alighted from the rickshaw. Transferring the basket of apples to the bicycle, which they wheeled along beside them, they began walking. The scent of the rice plants, fully ripened, was wafted powerfully to their nostrils. Annoyingly, locusts kept leaping around their feet. One, in panic-stricken flight, landed on Seki's shoulder, for a while becoming their road companion. Seki though, saying nothing, as if unaware that Sanjiro was even there, walked along with her eyes vaguely focused on a point in the far distance. Sanjiro suddenly felt that she had discerned a sort of vision there, that in looking at it she felt an intoxication like a swoon. Her eyes were too dreamy for it to be the lonely, crushed chagrin that Sanjiro felt. It was a very sweet dream, a sort of absentminded trance. Her emotion came home to Sanjiro with a peculiar clarity. The blood rose irresistibly into his cheeks. His heart pounded. The relations of G, said to be brimful of energy, and this beautiful body of Seki's, actually stirred up his sexual feelings with a strange power. In his imagination, it was no longer the lovemaking of others.

"Seki." His breath coming fast, he spoke in a gentle voice. "Last night, you weren't alone, were you? Somebody slept with you."

"At first, Yoshié-san slept next to me."

"And then?"

"After a while, Yoshié-san wasn't there any more. Mr G came in."

"And then?"

"Mr G said he'd been chased out by Yoshié-san and Mr. S."

"And then?"

". . ." Seki abruptly lowered her eyes.

All of a sudden, Sanjiro wanted to take Seki in his arms then and there. Seki was unbearably adorable. He began to be dangerously drawn in by his impulsive urge. Then, as if with a thud, he came back to himself. Astonished, he leapt away from his weird emotion.

"What kind of man are you?" he asked himself, then stopped, waiting for his feelings to calm down. A shallow emotion flowed into his heart, and he pitied Seki.

A while later, in a spot where there were woods on one side of the road and paddies on the other, leaning his bicycle against a telephone pole, Sanjiro relieved himself in the roadside weeds. It was a long piss. Happening to look up, about halfway up the pole he spotted something green. What was it, he thought, then recognized it for a rain frog. But why was it living in a telephone pole at the edge of the forest? In a small navellike cavity, rotted out around where a branch had grown when the pole was a standing tree in the mountains, a pair of frogs crouched one on top of the other. Sanjiro looked at them with an extraordinarily fond, affectionate emotion. A little above them, a rusted iron arm with a cobwebby bulb at its end overhung the road. The rain frogs had set up their modest household here to catch the insects that clustered around the bulb. Surely they were mates, Sanjiro thought. He pointed them out to Seki, but she displayed no interest whatsoever.

Shortly afterward, the couple arrived at the village. It was the same quiet, humble village of the day before. It was the same village that Sanjiro had left just a few hours earlier, and yet it seemed like a place that he hadn't seen in a very long time.

That evening, removing from the bookcase the four or five short story collections and the two collections of plays, Sanjiro carried them out unobserved by anyone to the trash pit on the mountainside behind the house. With a furtive timidity, as if he were doing something wrong, he burned them all and at last felt in the clear.

✲

✲

The House by the Moat

✲

One summer, I lived in the mountain-shadowed village of Matsué. I had a small house that faced on a moat at the edge of the village, perfect for living alone. From the garden, a stone stairs led right down to the moat. On the other side was a grove in back of the castle. The big trees, their trunks leaning, stretched their branches out low over the water. Water oats grew in the shallow water. Mellowed by age, the moat had more the air of an old pond. Little grebes, crying out, were always coming and going among the water oats.

Here I lived as simply as possible. When I came out here from my life in the city, drained dry by my relationships with people, people, people, it set my heart very much at ease. My life here was a relationship with insects, birds, fish, water, plants, the sky and, after them, lastly, with human beings.

When I came back late at night, several house lizards would have gathered by the light over my door. My house being the only one on this road with an eaves-light, it was a natural gathering place for the lizards of the neighborhood. Always with an uneasy sensation at the back of my neck, I hastily passed beneath them. Even with Nature, there were some relationships that were unwelcome. Elsewhere, if I had left the light on in the parlor, various insects would be attracted by that. Moths, beetles, and other light-seeking insects swarmed and swirled around the light bulb. Eyeing them, a number of bullfrogs crouched on the tatami. Startled by my tread, they would flee in the direction of the moat. But the leaf-frogs that clung to the houseposts, bending and twisting their bodies to the utmost, their golden eyes spinning, glared at this unexpected intruder who was myself. Actually, no doubt, I *was* an intruder, who had caused a panic in the house of frogs, lizards, and insects.

More or less driving out my visitors, I reclaimed the parlor as my own room. Then, I would start writing. At dawn, exhausted, I would crawl into bed. In the moat the carps and sunfish disported themselves in a lordly manner in the calm of daybreak. It was the spawning season just then. The fish vigorously leapt right out of the water, close by the bank. Listening to their splashing sounds, I would drop off to sleep.

By ten o'clock, it was already hot. I could not sleep any longer. When I got up, the woman next door whose garden was contiguous to mine would bring me live coals. I always left the earthen charcoal cooking brazier out in the garden under the damson tree. The housewife, bringing this charcoal from her own kitchen, without my asking her to, would fix up a fire, put on a brass kettle, and go back. When I'd wiped myself off with a wet towel, I would set about making breakfast. This consisted of bread and butter—the butter was the best, from the prefectural stock farm—black tea, a raw cucumber and, occasionally, radish pickle.

Previously, I had lived by myself in Onomichi. In the loneliness of being away from my family for the first time, I'd laid in an ample supply of household utensils for a homelike atmosphere. But after the experience of not actually using them at all, this time I meant to live as simply as I could.

Other than what I needed for tea and bread, I had no tableware. If I had a guest, I cooked beef sukiyaki in an enamel washbasin. I didn't feel this was especially unsanitary. On the contrary, it was when I used it as a washbasin that I got an unclean feeling. In the same bucket, I did my laundry, washed my cup and plate. When I boiled potatoes in the washbasin, I used the removable trapdoor from the kitchen as a lid.

Often my landlord, who liked to fish, would catch a lot of

carps and sunfish while I was still asleep. Stringing an eight- or nine-inch sunfish through the gills, as if tying up a dog, he would leave it alive in the moat for me. Chopping it up, I would feed it to the chickens next door.

The housewife's husband was a young carpenter. As it was apparently a slack season in his main trade, though, he devoted himself enthusiastically to his sideline of poultry raising. Since there was no boundary between our gardens, his chickens were always coming over to my side. When you attentively observed the life of the chickens, it was rather interesting. The very maternal demeanor of the mother hen, the innocent, childlike behavior of the chicks, the dignified mien, befitting the head of a family, of the rooster—all of them, each in character, each nicely suited to his or her place, made one life together. It was a pleasure to watch them.

When a Siberian black kite, which had flown up out of the castle grove, hovered low overhead, and the panic-stricken mother and her brood ran for cover under a tree or in the tall grass, the rooster, arrogantly opposing him alone, strutted in slow, stiff strides and worked himself into a battle fury.

Doing like their mother, the little chicks would scratch up the dirt. Then, lowering one tiny claw, they would pick up the kernel. When the mother hen showered herself with dust and sand, in unison all around her they too gave themselves a dust-bath. Things like these interested me. It was a particular pleasure to watch the shy, bustling, alert, and extremely lively activity of the hundred-day chicks with their bright yellow feet and fresh-colored cockscombs. It made you feel as if you were watching a cheerful, energetic young girl. Rather than beautiful, it was charming, lovable.

As, having my meal, I sat cross-legged on the veranda, invariably a black, ugly rooster with five or six females in tow would loiter about out front. I'd nicknamed him Kumasaka Chohan, after the famous bandit of ancient times. Reaching out his head, with a sort of speculation in the one eye that faced me, Kumasaka would glare in my direction. When I tossed him a bit of bread, although somewhat flustered, he would urgently call his hens and allow them to eat it. Quite cool and collected now, he would gobble down a crumb himself.

There was one day of violent wind and rain. In the dusky house with the shutters tightly closed, I was thoroughly bored. It was stuffy indoors, and I began to feel unwell. In the afternoon, finally making up my mind, I put on my shoes and a raincoat and went out into the storm. Without any destination, but not wanting to come back by the same road, I walked heedlessly alongside the railroad tracks, the rain splattering in my face, as far as the next station at Yumachi. The rain wet me through and through. Vapor arose from the openings in my coat. My stagnant mood, with the freshening of my circulation, changed completely for the better.

Some water lilies that I saw along the way in a reservoir pond were unbelievably beautiful. Steaming like smoke in the rain, from the wet gray color of the water's surface surrounded by a grove, their solitary white blossoms mistily shimmered and floated up to the eye. As flowers to look at in the wind and rain, I thought, there could be none lovelier than these.

About half a mile up into the mountains from Yumachi, there was a hot springs inn called Tamatsukuri. But a train came along just then that would take me home, so I turned back.

At the end of a lane in the Matsué neighborhood of Tonomachi, there was a restaurant run by a woman and her daughter. I was in the habit of having my supper at their place. So, on my way back, I went there.

Toward nightfall, the rain tapered off to a drizzle.

Borrowing a summer kimono, an umbrella, and a pair of high clogs, I left the restaurant. The rain had already stopped. Only the wind went on blowing. Almost without transition, the heavy weather of the day had turned into a pleasant, cool evening. Above the old, white-painted Western-style building of the produce display center, a pale, waning moon had dimly emerged.

Fleeting wisps of cloud were all being blown one way without pause.

With a pleasant tiredness and a full stomach, my mood, unusually for me, became calm and peaceful. I thought it would be too dull to spend the night working. I wanted to fall asleep slowly, in ease of spirit and body, while reading a good book.

When I got back, I spread out my bedding and lay down. Having nothing better around, I exposed my eyes to a half-read translation of a novel. I soon grew sleepy. But, thanks to my habit of working every night, when I thought I would fall asleep instead I became clear-eyed and wide awake. I could not get to sleep.

I don't know for how long I read that novel. All of a sudden, from the chicken coop next door, I heard the frantic squawks of chickens and the sound of something banging around inside the coop. Then I heard the shouts and screams of the carpenter and his wife as they came running from their house. Raising my head from the pillow, I listened intently. It must be a weasel or cat making a raid, I thought. The noise quickly died down. There were only the hens' clucking voices. The carpenter and his wife had a talk as they stood inside the chicken coop. After a while, though, they went back into their own house. Everything reverted to its original silence. Thinking "Well, so the chickens are safe," I soon dropped off to sleep.

The next day, the wind also had stopped. It was a beautiful clear day. As on every morning, when I opened the rain-shutters the carpenter's wife immediately came from next door bringing some live coals. When she saw the look on my face, she said:

"Last night, a cat did get one of our chickens."

". . ."

"It was a mother-hen . . . You know, if she'd been by herself she would have escaped. She was killed protecting her chicks."

"That's too bad."

"She was the mother of that bunch over there."

"What about the cat?"

"He got away."

"He did a cruel thing."

"Well, tonight we'll set a trap and catch him for sure."

"Will it be as easy as that?"

"We'll catch him. You'll see."

The chicks, cowering one and all in a dense patch of butterbur by the moat, uneasily popping out their heads in a row, peeped: "Pyo, pyo."

When I approached them, the chicks turned their faces toward me. But as soon as one of them got up, they all did. Stretching their heads out as far as they could and falling all over themselves, they fled.

"Can they grow up without a mother?"

"You might well ask."

"Won't some other hen take them under her wing?"

"No, she won't."

In fact, none of the other hens was the least bit kind to the orphaned chicks. Breaking up to mingle with another brood that had been born a short time before themselves, the chicks tried to squeeze in under the wings of the mother. Nervously pecking at their heads and tails, the hen chased them away. The chicks, with an air of wanting to depend on something, regrouped and looked about them uneasily.

The flesh of the killed chicken became that day's side dish for the carpenter and his wife. Only the head, its red wattles ripped to shreds and tatters, was thrown out into the garden. Its eyes half open, its beak slightly parted, it looked as if it had accepted its humiliation. Trembling with fear, the chicks gathered around it, but they did not seem to think it was the head of their mother. One chick started pecking at the exposed flesh of the neck like a cut-open pomegranate. Each time it was pecked, the head shifted its position on the sand. It'll be good if that cat gets caught nice and proper in the trap tonight, I thought.

Late that night, the cat did get caught in the trap in the desired manner. The carpenter and his wife, roused by the commotion, had come out and were talking about something in excited voices. With a straw rope, they tied the box that they had used as a trap more firmly shut from the top.

"It's all right to leave it this way. Tomorrow I'll submerge it in the moat, just so," I heard the carpenter say.

The couple went back into their house. Afterward, I stayed up and did some writing. But the voice of the cat, bucking around inside the box, got on my nerves with its caterwauling. When I thought that tonight was the cat's last night on earth, I felt sorry for him, but it seemed to me that there was nothing I could do.

When I thought that the cat had quieted down somewhat, he suddenly got angry again and banged back and forth inside the box, giving out a weird cry. "Gyaaa. Gyaa." The sound of him clawing at the sides of the box was irksome. But as I was thinking that that, too, would do him no good, this time the cat set up a pathetic, pleading yowl. "Miou. Miouu." The cat kept it up for a long while. By and by, drawn to take his side, I felt that I would like to help him out if I could.

When the cat had prolonged his cry to the bitter end, realizing that this too was not going to work, he lifted a barbaric howl of despair and started battering the sides of the box again. But then, at last, as if he had made up his mind that he was done for, he fell silent.

When I thought that the living creature that now drew breath in that crate over there would, at daybreak, be changed into a dead thing, it was not a good feeling. The cat and I were the only souls who were awake at this quiet late-night hour. It made me lonely to think that one of our two lives was doomed to be snuffed out at dawn. Wasn't killing the chicken something that the cat had had to do? It was very much in the natural order of things that a cat on his own should try to do so. For that very reason, people who raised chickens did what they had to do to prevent it. If, now and then, in a heavy rain, someone left the door open and the coop was raided, rather than regarding the cat as an evil pest it was truer to see it as the fault of the forgetful person. It would be good if, by a special act of grace, I were to let the cat go just this once. With a very different feeling from when I had looked at the chicks during the day, I thought about such things.

Actually, though, there was nothing to be done in the matter. I had the feeling that it was the sort of situation in which I could not raise a finger. At a time like this, I did not know what I should do. The chicks were to be pitied, and so was the mother hen. And now that the cat, who had caused their unhappy fate, had been caught, he too was unbearably pitiable. Moreover, it was a matter of course that my neighbors could not allow the cat to live. In fact, it seemed to me that there was not the slightest margin in which my feelings for the cat could go to work. I could only look on silently. I did not think that this was because of my heartlessness. If it was heartlessness, then the heartlessness of God was like this, I thought. If one wanted to, one could criticize a human being who was not God, who had free will, for looking on heartlessly as if he were God, but for me that course of events was like an irresistible destiny. I didn't even want to raise a finger.

The next day, when I woke up, the cat had already been drowned. His dead body had been buried. The box that had been used as a trap, set out in a sunny place, was already more than half dry.

✲

✲

A Memory of Yamashina

✲

When he came to the little stream of the Yamashina River, the moon was high and a cold wind was blowing across the harvested rice paddies. Finishing the cigarette he'd lit inside the car, he threw it away. Because of a qualm about riding in the car as far as the house, he'd gotten out on the Otsu highway and sent the woman back. As he walked, his mind was full of the woman whom he had just parted from. It was a pleasure, parting, to think about the beloved woman. It was a double pleasure. But, as he drew near the house, and the lie that he would have to tell his wife rose up before him, it became a dark perplexity that overshadowed him. Whenever he saw the lights of his house, that stood all alone on the other side, he experienced this perplexity. It even angered him that he was clearly in the position of the weaker party.

He loved his wife. Even when he'd fallen in love with the other woman, his love for his wife hadn't changed. But it was an extremely rare thing for him to love a woman other than his wife. And this rarity became a strong glamour; it lured and led him on. It seemed to him to lend a lively vitality to his stagnant life-mood. A selfish feeling, but not altogether a bad one, he thought.

Crossing the narrow earthen bridge, he entered the gate. At the sound of its little bell, he became afraid his cowardice would show itself. As casually as he could, he opened the wicket door and closed it behind him. What was it that darkened his feelings this way? It weighed on him to deceive his wife, who trusted him.

He slid open the glass door of the entryway, which caught all the light from inside. His wife, who usually came out right away, did not come out. Stepping up onto the house platform, he opened the sliding door there. In a corner of the room, in a rumpled heap of bedding like a pile of thrown away rags, bunched up in the sleeved coverlet, his wife lay huddled and small. He had never seen her like this. A strange sense of misery hit at his heart. Was this how he was treating his wife? Did his wife feel that she was treated like this? The feeling bludgeoned him. From the edge of the coverlet, drawn up over her head, his wife glared at him with one tear-bleary eye. The eye was smiling with mortification.

She knows everything, he thought. He grew excited, and angry. He silently glared back at his wife's eye. Until she said something, he could not speak a single word.

He turned on a light in the next room. In the round metal brazier, a well-kindled charcoal fire had been banked and kept alive. An iron teapot was on the boil.

"I thought something was wrong, somehow. When I called up, sure enough it was."

He didn't answer. Not taking off his inverness, he squatted by the brazier.

"Saying that kind of thing would never happen . . . telling pretty lies, deceiving others . . ." With this his wife got up and came into the room. He wanted to shout at her. But what was he to say? He could not find the words. With angry eyes, he studied his wife's face. It was a face smiling from utter mortification. But it had a strange reddish flush. Surely she has a fever, he thought.

"You're feverish," he said, putting a hand to his wife's forehead when she'd sat down by his side. Roughly brushing off his hand, she answered:

"I don't care if I do have a fever."

Even to a light touch, she felt feverish. Getting up, he took the padded kimono that had been laid out on his bed roll and made her put it on.

His wife was in earnest. Her eyes, which usually did not shine with much energy, were glittering. She looked straight into his eyes. He felt as if he'd flinched at that look. But, making his voice strong, he said:

"It's no concern of yours. It has nothing to do with you."

"What? Doesn't it have everything to do with me? Why does it have nothing to do with me?"

"If you hadn't found out about it, it wouldn't have been your concern. My feeling for you is not the least bit different because of such a person." He was aware that what he was saying was willful. But since he already loved the other woman, he could only feel happy that there had been no change in his love for his wife.

"That's not it. That's not it at all. We used to be one, but now we've split into two. All you think about is going to that place."

"Feelings aren't like arithmetic."

"No. That's not what I think."

His wife, growing hysterical, slapped the back of his hand.

He told her once again that he did not feel the least bit unfaithful to her.

"If you hadn't felt unfaithful, it's not likely that kind of thing would have happened, is it?"

But he was not telling a falsehood. It displeased him that, whatever he said, he would be trying to rationalize the unreasonable.

"It's not as if I'll feel this way all my life. As long as I don't make you unhappy with it, it's all right."

"But you do make me unhappy. I've never felt unhappiness like this." Even during the worst of their poverty, she had borne up under it. Only to this, no matter how much time went by, she would never be able to resign herself.

"Haven't I always said that? As long as you don't become unhappy at this late hour, it's all right. How can you say such a thing?"

For him, there was justification in the fact that his feelings toward the woman were serious. But for his wife, the more serious they were the more impermissible they were. He'd had a hazy hope that she who by nature could be rather magnanimous, whatever the matter, might also show a spirit of forgiveness in this, his affair, but after all it was impossible. It was also impossible to talk to her much about his feelings for the woman. And so, as his wife's hysteria mounted, he had nothing to say.

For five minutes, they were silent. They thought their own thoughts. Now and then, the thought of the woman passed through his mind.

"Last year, when I was in the hospital, I thought it would be terrible if I fell in love with that doctor. Even though truly I was happy just thinking of you." Somewhat calmer now, his wife suddenly said this.

"H'm." He had a strange feeling. He could clearly remember that young man, whom his wife had respectfully addressed as "Sensei."

"I know. That Doctor What's-his-name. I wrote a story about it."

". . . " Abruptly putting on a serious face, his wife looked steadily at him. He could not really grasp his wife's feeling. He only felt for certain that there was nothing impure in it.

"What were you going to say?"

". . . But that was something completely different from Daddy's feelings. Unless you understand that, it's no good."

"I don't think mine are any different. But I don't think, either, that your feelings were unfaithful."

Standing up, he took a notebook from his worktable. "There's a woman called A. She's a good wife and a wise mother. But, just once in her life, without clearly knowing it, she felt a love for another man that made her heart pound. Only her husband, and the other man, were aware of this. There were no opportunities, and nothing happened. Her love had come and gone. Even the woman A has forgotten about it. There's a woman called B. She fell in love the same way. But she did not even know about it herself." "B" was his wife.

"Take a look. 'A' is ———."

His wife innocently accepted the notebook, but did not try to read it.

"But, it's strange," his wife said, with an expression as if she were examining her emotions. "If I'd had the least feeling of shame, I wouldn't have told Daddy about it."

Actually, when he'd gone to visit her, his wife had buoyantly prattled on about the man.

"That's so."

"It is so. I think my feeling was that even Daddy would be pleased he was being so good to me."

"But your thinking it would be terrible if you fell in love was about the doctor, wasn't it? I thought that just as I wrote in here you didn't even know that much."

". . ."

"You entered on the sixteenth of April. May, June, July, August, September, October, November, December—for eight months, you didn't touch on the matter, so I didn't think much about it myself. If there had been the makings of anything unpleasant in it, you're not the sort of person who could have remained silent. I didn't think there were any. I didn't have the slightest feeling of jealousy. Rather, I felt sorry for you somehow. I was well aware of the nature of your feelings. After you left the hospital, too, both Miss ——— and I said that if it was just to have the dressing changed you could go to a doctor around here. But you wouldn't listen."

His wife interrupted him.

"That's not true. I was thinking of ———san in Abiko. The doctor's office here seemed dirty to me. I thought it would be awful if after it had finally healed germs were to get into it again, and I said so. It's a bit too much, if you're even going to take things like that amiss."

"Well, I don't know what the truth is, but I think even Miss ——— took it that way. She made a face, and looked at me. I didn't want to make a thing of it, so I let you have your way. But I could see that without knowing it you were dominated by those feelings of yours."

"That may be so . . . I don't think so, but . . ."

"It's not just I who think so. I believe the other person was aware of it also."

"If that's so, why didn't you come out and say that I was not to go to the hospital? I don't think I felt that way, but if you thought I did, why didn't you stop me? Daddy was bad."

"First of all, I didn't think you would get into any trouble. Even if you did, I knew that anything like that was a very long ways down the road. And even the fact that I was not someone who could rest easy about such a thing was a source of relief. I'm sure that my repugnance to saying something too strong came from that alone."

As he said this, he only now realized what extraordinary leeway he'd allowed in the matter. The purity of his wife's feelings had been reflected in himself, he thought.

The doctor was a lively, congenial young man. He had spoken with him only a few times, but had had no bad feelings about him. Often, when he'd entered his wife's sickroom, the doctor had hurried out past him. His wife was especially cheerful at such times. Once, when their youngest girl was staying over, she'd suddenly begun to cry and scream in the dead of night, saying she wanted to go home. His wife had unexpectedly arrived in a taxi with the girl. The young doctor had granted permission, on condition that she return for an examination in the morning. His wife had laughed, telling how the doctor had teased her. Early in the morning, she'd gone back by taxi again.

Though he didn't think the doctor had designs on her, he felt the man knew as well as himself what her feelings were.

At the time of her release, there had been a question of whether to make out-patient visits. Finally, with a glum face, his wife had agreed to have the dressing changed by a doctor in Yamashina. When, the next day, she'd gone to that doctor, his office had been unusually clean so that she'd been glad of her decision.

It was lucky that the conversation had shifted to his wife's affair. His wife was calm now. But that was no help in eliciting the slightest leniency toward his own affair. She obstinately held firm, until he promised to break with the woman. In this alone, she was strong.

There was nothing to do but to acquiesce, if only for the time being.

✲

✲

Infatuation

✲

It was a cold, thinly overcast day. With a slight headache from the chill and feeling much depressed, he'd shut himself up in his study. From time to time snow had been falling, hiding the mountains beyond. There was a pond in the garden, and the snow would quickly fall and disappear in it. As he looked through the panes of the shoji and the glass outer door, the snow stopped and blue sky appeared. It was typical mountain weather.

He could not make up his mind what to do in this affair. It would be best to give up the woman, but he disliked that idea as having come from his wife. The woman herself felt no affection for him. If he came to feel nothing for her and they quietly separated, well and good. But he could not steel himself to the forced obedience of leaving her now, although for a while he had meant to. Nevertheless it was disagreeable to go on deceiving his wife, who for her part had been magnanimous in the affair. If he added this to all the previous considerations, it was clearly an impossible situation. It would have been ideal, of course, had it been possible for *him*. He had even gone so far as to suggest the possibility the night before, but had immediately realized that it was a hopeless venture.

His wife had asked him to settle the affair today. She was in earnest. He could not compete with her sincerity. He had thought that he was being unusually serious himself but was far behind his wife in this respect.

At any rate, he had decided that a short, formal separation was the only answer. His wife's saying that it could be done with money, though, unpleasantly revealed her contempt for the woman. He could not easily stomach it. No doubt she spoke the truth, and he might have said the same of another person. But it was unlike his wife to say it. He understood that she spoke as one who had been betrayed and cheated, but it annoyed him nonetheless.

Even after he'd fallen in love with the woman, his feelings toward his wife had in no way changed. Rather, his wife had continued to derive a charm from the thought of the torment he inflicted by deceiving her. But now that things between them had come down to such a blank openness, even this gave him only a dry, chilled feeling. To have changed so suddenly—if only for a while—seemed the act of a coward.

The woman was a waitress in a Gion teahouse. A big-boned, mannish girl of twenty or so, she had no such spiritual problems. It was strange even to him how he could have been so attracted to her. Her beauty belonged to a type he liked, but it astonished him that he had been so deeply drawn to her.

There was a savor in this girl, long since lost in his wife, of a fresh fruit. Her breath was as fragrant as any child's. Her flesh was like the pure white meat of a crab caught in northern seas. So far as all these were the charms of a physical fascination, his was a vulgar emotion; and yet, in the passion by which he was endlessly drawn to her, beyond so-called dissipation, he could see nothing but love. Having its own beauty, even that which was ugly in her did not seem ugly to him.

His thoughts made him grimace to himself. Just then his wife, all the more excited for being overstimulated and tired, came into the room.

"Isn't it getting late for the bank?"

"Won't tomorrow do as well?"

"No. You must take care of it today. The longer it's put off the longer I suffer. I should never have let you think it was your own affair. It's past one. I have things to do myself. Please get ready now."

"You should stay indoors."

"No. I cannot sit at home."

"But don't you have a fever?"

"It would be nice if I got sick, wouldn't it? Got sick and died—isn't that what you really want?"

He glared up at her.

"Stop talking about things you don't understand—even as a joke."

"'Things I don't understand'—is that how little it means to you?"

"It's not a question of life and death."

"I wonder."

"Only a fool would lump them together."

"That doesn't mean they *aren't* together."

He was aware that what she said as his wife could not invariably be dismissed as overstatement, and yet it angered him.

"Are you threatening me? It's vulgar to try and control people's actions that way."

His wife was silent. He'd spat out the venomous words just as they came to him.

Paling, his wife looked at him intently and then lowered her eyes. Sighing, she said:

"You really are selfish."

"I have always acted on my desires."

"Yes, I knew you always did as you pleased. But to completely deceive me with that as your excuse, and then to nonchalantly accuse me of coercion and vulgarity—how do you do it? You're shrewdly penetrating when you judge others, but for yourself the rules are quite different. Why do you think that is? People who scold their children for telling lies don't mind their own, it seems."

"If it were good to tell you the truth I would, always. If you could stand the truth I would always tell it to you."

"That's not what I heard before. Are you getting desperate for things to say?"

It was unbearably disagreeable. He did not want to go on.

"What you said then was good. You did tell me all the truth last night? You aren't hiding anything from me? Give me your firm promise that you will never do this kind of thing again—allow me at least to believe that. I will forget everything that has happened up to now. Please let me believe that much . . . Well?"

"I can't promise anything. Unexpected things have come up. I can't undertake for the future."

"In that case I can't go on living."

There was a note of hysteria in his wife's voice.

"What will you do, if you can't go on living?"

"I don't intend to kill myself, but it will come to the same thing. It can turn out no other way."

With his wife in this state, he would have to temporarily break with the woman. The thought irked him.

After an hour's ride, they got off in Kyoto at Higashiyama-sanjo. Large, abundant snowflakes were falling. It was a good feeling. The sun had been shining when they left Yamashina, and they hadn't brought umbrellas. Their heads and shoulders exposed to the snow, they stood cringing from the windblown flakes. The street whitened as they watched.

"I'll be back in an hour or so. You wait for me at our friend's house. We must be as calm as possible about this."

His wife silently looked into his eyes.

"It's cold—you should go there quickly. Are you warm enough?"

His wife nodded.

"So. Until then."

Leaving her, he decided to walk the short distance rather than take the crowded trolley. Crossing the narrow street, he went into a shop to buy cigarettes. When he came out his wife was still standing there, her hair and breast covered with snow. Looking as if she were about to cry, she seemed to say something in a low voice. She had noticeably weakened in a single day. When he went up to her, she laid her head on his shoulder and, as if appealing to him, said:

"It's all right, isn't it?"

"Yes, of course. If you stay out in this snow you really will get sick."

His wife finally went back. Her small head, with its bound coiffure perched on top of the thick shawl, seemed quite drab and pathetic.

Entering the place where he and the woman always met, he found the madam sitting at an oblong brazier in the darkened tearoom. She got up slowly. "A heavy snowfall." There was something lazy and catlike about her.

"Something has come up. She'll be in shortly."

The woman came almost immediately. When he told her she looked puzzled and was silent. At last she said: "No, I can't." Congratulatory presents had been received from all the geishas—she could not do it on such short notice. Her reasons were clear. The woman seemed genuinely disconcerted because of them. She began to cry.

"You don't have to make an announcement, do you?"

"It would soon be known."

"Probably it would be best if I went away."

He had no confidence that if he stayed in Kyoto he would not come here. It really would be as well if he left, he thought. When he said so, the woman replied: "No, don't." She turned her dull, tear-stained face toward the window. Her expression was merely one of vague melancholy.

He took the woman's big, heavy body onto his knees. Her lips were brackish from her tears. He thought of the similarly salty taste of his wife's mouth the night before, and how unlike him it was to be involved with two women.

After a while, paying the bill and giving the woman money, he left. Outside it was still snowing in flurries.

The friend's house was on the grounds of a large temple west from where they'd gotten off the trolley. As he went in by the back gate he met his wife coming out.

"It was awkward just sitting there talking," she said as if apologizing. She looked up at him. "It's all settled, then?"

"Yes." He nodded. The weakness of his acquiescence bothered him.

On the face of it, he supposed, everything was settled. But the problem of his feelings was far from resolved. When the woman had asked him to come once more before he went away, he'd given her a vague answer. For himself, he had not the slightest wish to leave her. Everything had been settled, as his wife said, and yet it had not. Instead of deceiving his wife, he was now deceiving himself. If he was not deceiving himself, by acting in this way he deceived his wife anew and the woman as well. He was reluctant to deal with the problem squarely if it meant wrecking his domestic arrangements. Besides, he didn't think it mattered that much. The woman had disliked him at first. Although she didn't dislike him now, he knew, without his wife telling him, that for her it was not more than a transaction. This attitude of hers was not pleasant for him, but in her world it was morality. Even supposing that she loved him, it would be impossible for her to leave such calculation entirely behind her.

Nevertheless, he could not keep her out of his head alone or in company. He could not bring himself to break with her until he had, in some sense, made his peace with her.

The rest of that day, he and his wife walked around the city. In the evening they went back to Yamashina. From that night on his wife was sick. It had been wrong for her to go out with a fever.

Although his wife's illness was merely a cold, it refused to clear up.

"I feel much better now that things have been taken care of."

He was perplexed when she spoke this way. His answers were meant to reassure her but their tone was not cheerful. It was not easy to be cheerful with his wife so anxious to believe him.

Once they had this conversation:

"It's after all like an illness in the family, one which will leave no trace. But it will mean a shorter life . . ."

"An illness, you say. That doesn't mean you won't catch it again," he replied, turning it off as a joke. He found it simpler to talk this way.

At any rate, he wanted to get away quickly. He did in fact have business in Tokyo, but his wife's illness lingered on strangely and he could not leave her so. More serious than the illness itself was his wife's nervous condition. She was always more or less in a state of febrile agitation. Her plain wedding ring, which usually seemed embedded in the plump flesh, now slid off easily when she lowered her hand.

The following is a letter he received from his wife not long after, when he was in Tokyo.

I am glad to hear you are well. Since you left it has snowed every day, and is bitterly cold. Are you looking after your neuralgia? I worry about you all—glad to hear you're in good spirits. I meant to thank you for the present but haven't had a chance to write. Thank you, very much. Please forgive me for being my usual weak-minded self when you left. It wasn't at all that I was depressed, but I was in bed and not feeling well. Just now I was crying by myself, and so began this letter. I mustn't bother him, I thought, and held off as long as I could. But it became too much for me, and here I am writing you these silly things. When I'm alone I think about it and the tears start to come. It's over and done with, I think, but I can't help myself. I just cannot feel cheerful about it. Please don't make me suffer like this ever again. The monkey died after all. Even now I can't bear the sadness of it. I truly believe you. It was because I did believe you that this has happened. It's bad for us to keep things from each other. I am merely expressing a selfish wish and it may offend you, but I beg of you—my suffering begs of you. You said that I mean something to you—it's disgraceful of me to feel so gloomy, but when I think of what happened I forget what you said. It makes me terribly sad. Thank you for your letter in which you explain everything. It set my heart at rest.

I imagine you every day hard at work on your writing. Please take good care of yourself—don't catch cold. If your neuralgia is even slightly worse you should go to the hot springs at Hakone for it. I'm glad you got the warm clothes I sent after you. Nothing in particular to report about our evenings here. The children are well. I've stopped crying so much. Sometimes when I'm depressed and get to thinking the tears still come. I'm trying as hard as I can to cheer myself up. You said that you love me, so whatever happens I won't be afraid. It's only my selfishness—if I weren't alone, my nerves wouldn't act up so. Please forgive me for not having considered your feelings, and writing only about myself. But just writing this trivial letter has made me feel better. My love to you all.

He'd gotten back from a walk and was reading this when a telegram came. PLEASE RETURN. His wife's loneliness, which she could not bear any longer, welled up powerfully in him. He thought it was good that she hadn't tried to bear it any longer. Although his business was not nearly finished, he decided to go back at once.

"Is she still sick, do you think?"

"No. It's because I've had another woman."

His mother did not answer. "I should go back right now."

He packed in twenty minutes, and was in time for the last express.

✲

✲

Kuniko

✲

Whatever I say, Kuniko's having committed suicide is my responsibility. I do not think of trying to deny that. But for me, that was something that I could have done almost nothing about. Of course, if I'd known that she was going to kill herself, I would have thought about how to prevent it. But I never thought it was that kind of thing. That was my negligence. But there were sufficient reasons for such negligence. I didn't even dream that I was treating Kuniko so harshly that she had to kill herself. I truly loved Kuniko. Probably it is incomprehensible to others how Kuniko, whom I loved, could have killed herself, leaving three children. From the outside, it must seem that either I treated Kuniko atrociously or that Kuniko, without meaning to, killed herself in a moment of impulse. But neither conclusion is correct. Truly, I loved Kuniko from my heart. I cannot think that Kuniko herself did not believe that. But once Kuniko was dead, I came to feel for the first time that her death was after all inevitable.

In the final analysis, I killed Kuniko, but I cannot bear to actually think so. Yet since Kuniko's death, I have come to think of nothing else. I've come to feel that no matter how much I castigate my foolishness I can never finish. But there is more to it than merely feeling remorse. What were Kuniko's emotions when she killed herself? That is what I've thought about. I am utterly unable to grasp what they were. "No one has yet exactly described the feelings of the suicide himself." Thus it is written in the note of a certain suicide,* and it is all the more to be

*Akutagawa Ryunosuke, the writer, committed suicide early on the morning of July 24, 1927. (translator's note)

expected that I, who am not the person concerned, should be unable to grasp such feelings. However, since I am a playwright, whose business is writing, it won't do merely to castigate my own foolishness and wrap myself in a cocoon of remorse. I intend to write about my misfortune (not saying "Kuniko's," I dare to say "my"). I will be satisfied if by the act of writing I am able to put even somewhat in order the various thoughts that are smouldering murkily in my head. I do not in the least aim to justify myself by this writing. But if in this way I am able to castigate myself accurately, my feelings might be resolved.

Kuniko had always had a sad life. As a child, she was brought up in poverty that although not actual beggary was close to it. When, in the spring of the year before last, my eldest boy nearly died of pneumonia, the nurse took extraordinarily good care of him. Kuniko did not know how to show her gratitude. Then, on the day of the celebration of his complete recovery, she gave the nurse a pearl ring that was her most precious possession, and was finally able to satisfy herself. When a play of mine had first been performed, Kuniko had asked me for this pearl ring to remember the occasion by.

"It's all right, isn't it? I know it's unfair to you, but I feel that unless I give her this very ring she won't know how grateful I am." As if wheedling me, Kuniko said this kind of thing.

"If it makes you feel good, it's all right."

"Thank you. And I'll tell Miss Kitamura. That it's a ring with a history."

"You don't have to tell her that kind of thing."

"No, I'll tell her. Because if I don't, my feeling won't get through to her."

It was at this time that Kuniko told me the following story:

Every year, on the day of the grand summer cleaning, Kuniko and her mother would go through the town, culling out old clogs, old fans, rags, and glass bottles and the like from the piles of trash heaped high in front of the houses. Kuniko, shouldering the big bundle that was too much for a child of five or six to carry, assiduously poking with a bamboo pole among such things under the eaves of the houses with her mother, did not feel sorry for herself or anything like it. Rather, as a regular annual event, she remembered it as one of her pleasures. One time, Kuniko came across a little ring in the trash. She thought she had discovered something of great value. The stone was a ruby, although of course it was nothing but red glass, the sort of thing that sold in haberdasheries at the time for ten or fifteen sen. But her joy when she found it was many times greater than when she'd received this pearl ring.

"It's unforgivable of me to say this kind of thing, but I'm telling you the truth." Apologizing, Kuniko went on. Although she took very good care of this peerless treasure, just two or three days later the German silver clasps that held the stone in place loosened, and the stone fell out. Kuniko was heartbroken, and cried and cried without coming to the end of her tears.

"This is not the kind of story I can tell to others, but I will never forget it as long as I live."

Kuniko lost her mother, the only parent she knew, when she was thirteen. At that time, by knitting argyle socks on a little hand-operated loom, they were beginning to be somewhat better off, but after terrible suffering from cancer of the rectum the mother finally died. Child though she was, Kuniko fully realized that she was now on her own in life. From something exceptional in her, a neighbor offered to send her to a geisha house as an apprentice. But there were others to help Kuniko, and she went to a certain family as a nursemaid. After that, she also worked as a factory girl and as a waitress in a railway station restaurant.

I first met Kuniko when she was working at a summer resort in the mountains. My impression of her was that her fingernails were as dirty as her face was beautiful. Every day, as she put out the plates, those hands irritated me. On one hand there was a plain wedding ring, but although I sensed some attachment there, I thought nothing of it. I couldn't tell whether it signified that she was already married or meant an engagement. Probably it was more of a charm against misfortune, I thought.

At any rate, I regarded this woman with a neutral feeling, although I cannot say, of course, that my feelings were entirely virtuous. Already thirty-six, I was still a bachelor. The feelings of such a man—a man habituated to insincerity toward women—when, without love, he looks at a beautiful woman and especially a woman who may be available, are not all they should be. In that respect I was no different from most other men. But I didn't feel enough of an urge to try positively to make the thing happen.

One night, tired from writing, I left off at a place from which it didn't seem as if I could get any further. But my mind went on working, and I thought I would change my mood bedward by twenty or thirty minutes of billiards. It was already after eleven o'clock. Treading softly, out of consideration for the other guests, I walked down the long hallway towards the billiards room.

From the hallway you went up two or three steps into a narrow corridor, then down again and into the billiards room. On the left side of that corridor, there were two guest rooms that were used only when the hotel was crowded. From one room, I heard a man and woman having an argument in low voices. Nobody passed along this corridor except to go to the billiards room, and the hour was late. To be sure, the relationship between the man and woman did not seem to be an innocent one, but having come this far I could not abruptly turn back. From the tone of their voices, the man seemed to be pressing the woman, who was refusing. Deliberately making a normal sound of footsteps, I was about to pass by their room when, slamming back the half-opened sliding door, a woman in a summer kimono and an under sash, evidently fresh from her bath, suddenly jumped out. Her face an ugly red with excitement, it was Kuniko. Since the door was open, naturally I saw into the room. A young waiter who worked in the same hotel restaurant was sitting on the bed. His eyes full of malevolence, he glared at me. I kept going, down into the billiards room.

The next morning, I felt nervous about seeing the pair when I went down to breakfast. Assuming the girl was all right, the man probably would not have the face to look at me, I thought. If it were possible, I wanted to tell him: "It's no great matter. Don't worry. I won't tell anyone." Actually, I liked that young waiter. His figure as he strode down the corridor energetically banging the dinner gong was an image of youth itself. He was courteous in his treatment of the guests, and intelligent. Besides, for a young person in the mountains for the summer, that kind of thing seemed unavoidable. Especially when it had ended in failure, it was nothing to find fault with.

When I went downstairs that morning—what had happened?—neither of the two was in attendance. Then another waitress, as she brought my dishes to the table, a faint smile dimpling in her cheeks as she looked at me, tacitly showed me that she too knew of the affair.

That morning, the young waiter was dismissed and sent down the mountain.

At lunch, Kuniko made her appearance. Serving tables far away from mine, though, she contrived as much as possible not to look at me. Having my tea brought out onto the veranda, I was smoking a cigarette and gazing at the distant mountains when Kuniko, red-faced, came up to me and murmured:

"About last night, thank you very much."

Politely bowing her head, she immediately withdrew. Indeed, I had inadvertently practiced secret charity towards Kuniko, but I thought it too bad if the boy had had to be dismissed because I knew of the matter. Perhaps, I thought, Kuniko had made it public precisely because they'd been seen by me.

After this occurrence, the relationship between me and Kuniko gradually grew closer. But our sexual relations did not begin until half a year later, when Kuniko was working at a certain café in Shiba and I made up my mind to approach her. It wasn't too difficult for a man like me to take up with a woman from that sort of place, but our relationship until then having been rather too mannerly, it required a certain leap to make the proposition. "I truly was saved that time, thanks to you." When she said things like this, Kuniko was excessively serious. "Do you feel yourself indebted to me?" I went so far as to say this, but it was difficult to go further and say: "If that is so, then . . ." Good boy that I was, I was unable to broach the matter. Thus it took half a year to break through. Of course, during that time, I was not always going to that café. I went once or perhaps twice a week. The expression that appeared on Kuniko's face the moment I entered gradually attracted me. Kuniko was in love with me. That sort of self-conceit was one of my characteristics, but it was a fact that Kuniko trusted me and was happy to see me. That much at least I clearly felt, and naturally it made my feelings serious. So it became harder and harder to make the leap, but finally I did. It was because my feelings had already come down on one side. Initially frivolous, they had turned into love. From a lie, truth had been born.

After a while, we decided to live together. Rather than Tokyo where many people knew her, Kuniko wanted to live in the suburbs, so, finding a suitable house for rent in Kichijo-ji, we moved there.

For the previous three years, I'd lived in Takagi-cho in Aoyama with an old housekeeper. But even household furnishings which until then had been perfectly adequate, when Kuniko came, were apt to be wanting in one way or another. We often went shopping in such department stores as Mitsukoshi and Shirokiya for furniture for our new household.

Two years earlier, Kuniko had been a kept woman. The man was the head clerk of a stock brokerage, and at first had been rather generous. Once Kuniko was his mistress, though, he suddenly turned into an extraordinary miser. Kuniko had no particular objections to his stinginess, but, while loath to give her anything at all, he made extreme and violent demands on her body, such that it hardly seemed the treatment of a human being. Kuniko grew to hate the man deeply. Moreover the man was exorbitantly jealous. At first, thinking that jealousy is a face of love, Kuniko did not altogether take offence at it. Gradually, though, it became clear that his secret intention was to make that a pretext for letting her go without giving her any money. That excessively ugly calculation made Kuniko furious. Unable now to bear being kept a day longer, Kuniko herself made the break, coming away from the man with empty hands. After the break, however, the man, seeming to feel some lingering regret for her, often came to the café and tried to take her out. But Kuniko would have nothing more to do with him.

Kuniko's room was more or less furnished by now. Looking around at it, and remembering the meager, cheap articles that had been allotted to her in the other house, even now Kuniko felt anger.

"You won't be cross with me? I want to tell you how happy I am. Up to now, I couldn't even imagine this kind of happiness."

Mounting in a thin silver frame a photograph of a foreign beauty holding a fluffy white cat—a Persian cat, I believe—and rubbing her cheek against it, Kuniko hung it on the wall. To my taste, the thing belonged on the wall of a barber shop, but I didn't have the heart to disillusion Kuniko, who took such pleasure in it, so I remained silent. Rather than call attention to her bad taste, I thought I would regard her naiveté as leniently as possible. The furniture, too, was not in such good taste as to merit Kuniko's transports, but if it made her happy it was all right, I thought.

We led a life for all the world like that of a newly married couple. Thinking of my age, I had a strange feeling. The two of us were the perfect lovers.

There were awkward moments, such as when the old woman would abruptly slide open the opaque paper door.

"Those two certainly go at it. I'm afraid to open a door in this house," the old woman would mumble, loud enough for us to hear.

The old woman and Kuniko did not get on well at all. The old woman's family had originally been temple samurai. I don't know whether it was true or not, but deliberately letting it be known that she had been raised by a wet nurse and under parasols, she implicitly tried to remind Kuniko that she was an ex-café waitress. Kuniko wept tears of mortification. I was angered myself, but since she was not directly showing contempt I could not even scold the old woman.

When it had been just the two of us, she was not all that much the old woman. It was strange how when Kuniko came, she suddenly changed. She thought me weak to have brought an ex-waitress into the house. Even her attitude toward me became somehow arrogant. And then—this happened often when I was out—she liked to minutely correct something that Kuniko was especially doing for me. "When the master lived alone, we did it this way," she would say. When I asked, there were times when that was so, but there were also times when it was not so. I came to think that if the old woman, to whom I owed nothing, was going to endlessly make scenes like this, it was foolish to torment Kuniko by keeping her on in my employ. But she had been serviceable in the past, and I was loath to get angry and fire her. While I was hesitating, finally Kuniko herself lost patience with her and broke things open between them. "That is not my job," the old woman declared haughtily. "Fine, then why don't you leave," Kuniko replied.

Emphasizing that although I recognized her services hitherto, now that things had come to this pass I had no choice but to ask her to leave, I finally dismissed the old woman.

Kuniko frequently showed her supreme satisfaction with this life of ours. She repeatedly said that she had never imagined that this kind of happiness could come into her life. I was happy myself, and the thought that I had made Kuniko so happy returned to me as an increase of happiness. There was a sentimental feeling about our life, but I didn't think of turning cynical eyes on that sentimentality.

Before long, Kuniko was pregnant. Uneventful days passed,

and a boy was born. The birth was extraordinarily easy, but after a month Kuniko began to complain that she did not quite feel herself. I had the doctor look at her, and it turned out that some of the placenta, which we thought had completely descended, was still inside her. On account of that, Kuniko spent a month in a hospital near Suruga.

A second child was born. Several uneventful and excessively peaceful years passed. Rejoicing in them, Kuniko experienced true happiness. For Kuniko, then, busy every day with things concerning the children, there was no boredom. But sometimes I couldn't stand the boredom and even began to lose my temper. My burdensome task of organizing a theater group, which I was doing in addition to my play-writing, became too much for me. On top of the boredom that was killing me, I felt as if the press of business was killing me a second time. Now and then I was tempted to have an affair, but I always held back and declined the offer. Everything gradually became dreary.

Soon, a little incident occurred that put a dent in Kuniko's happiness.

I had a brother who was ten years older than I. He was a teacher at a school in the Kansai region. One day, I received a telegram from his wife saying to please come at once. What is it? I wondered. Usually, in instances of this kind, the telegram would come in my brother's name. It was strange that this time it had come from his wife. With a vague premonition of bad luck, I left that night on the express.

What had happened was that my brother was having a casual affair with the servant girl. The girl was giving herself airs in trivial matters over my brother's wife.

"It's not that I'm jealous. Your brother tells me not to mind that kind of trivial affair, but Fuji sometimes does arrogant things to me. They make me angry . . . because it's not something that a teacher ought to do. I feel unbearably ashamed for Takiko's sake. It's truly unpardonable of me to have asked you to come so far, but I'd like you to have a good talk with your brother."

"I don't know what to say. I can understand if you're angry with my brother, but I feel slightly guilty about offering him advice. Because I'm not qualified to. When I was single I caused my brother a good deal of embarrassment in such matters."

"That's why I thought it would sound better coming from you."

"That's true, but . . . are you certain he's having an affair?"

"Well, I haven't seen them in the act, but there's no question of it. At any rate, it makes me unbearably angry to have Fuji living with us and making big faces. I don't say anything to your brother about his relationship with Fuji. I tell him to dismiss her immediately."

"My brother doesn't agree to that?"

"No."

"Does Takiko know about it?"

"I wonder, now. She's a carefree child, so she may not have noticed anything."

Takiko, my brother's only daughter, was now in her third year of girls' school. My brother loved her very much.

That afternoon, my brother finished his classes and came home. Apparently thinking it strange that I was there, he asked me when and why I had come. But he soon seemed to realize that his wife had sent for me.

Although his wife had requested me to, I could not bring myself to speak directly to my brother about that sort of thing.

That evening, I called Takiko into the parlor and said:

"Do you know why Uncle has come this time?"

". . ." At a loss for an answer, Takiko reddened and looked aside.

"Evidently you do know. That's perfectly all right, but don't say anything about it to your father. Just say: "Please dismiss Fuji." Your father will certainly not ask 'Why?' Is that all right? Do you understand?"

I thought it was somewhat cowardly of me, but it was the best I could do.

And it succeeded as I thought it would. My brother's simple acquiescence gave me a very good feeling. He's not a fool after all, I thought.

Coming back on the train, I was sorely perplexed as to how to tell this story to Kuniko. It was out of the question to tell her nothing—she'd been sitting at home worrying all this while. Although there was no particular necessity to conceal the matter from her, if I told her this story I might end up confessing that I'd done the same thing myself. That pained me. It was already a thing of the past, and by now would not bother Kuniko in the least, but . . .

When Kuniko had been in the hospital having our first child, I had committed that kind of indiscretion two or three times with a beautiful maid we had then. Due to personal circumstances of her own, the girl had left my house before Kuniko came home from the hospital. Having managed to get out of the affair scot-free, I had almost forgotten about it by now. But if I told her my brother's story—if Kuniko, feeling displeasure at such a thing, sympathized with my brother's wife, and surely she would sympathize—I would be totally unable to wipe my mouth and look innocent about what I had done. And yet I flinched at the dreadful, mean cruelty of disappointing Kuniko, who believed steadfastly that since our marriage I had become a completely honest man in that regard.

When I got home, I hadn't decided whether to tell her or not to tell her. But in the end I did tell her. The same blood flowed in my brother and myself. To tell her one side, and omit the other side of the story, gave me an extremely bad feeling. I could not bear to do it.

Kuniko was horribly surprised. Having built up an illusion that we were a so-called good family, she was sufficiently shocked just to hear of my brother's affair. Being told of mine along with it apparently made her feel as if she'd suddenly been pushed off a cliff.

"It's something that happened in the past, so it should be all right, but I'm truly disappointed. Because I believed completely in you. Why are men that way? Both you and your brother are good persons. Why do you do that kind of thing? Somehow the world seems dark gray now. When I was at that café, I saw absolutely all sorts of people, but I thought that kind of person was an animal. Then when I met you, I felt that you were a person of a completely different world from such people. That was why I respected you and naturally fell in love with you. Why did you . . ."

"Stop it," I told her, unable to take any more. "You overestimated me. Weren't you well aware that when I was single I did a lot of that kind of thing? During that time, I was a companion of your 'animals.' And I can't say even now that I'm not. I'm not trying to absolve myself, but most men have that 'animal' in them. The only difference is whether to let it roam free or bind it with chains. . . . To put it strongly, that 'animal' *is* man."

"Ah, I can't bear any more. That's the first time I've heard you say such terrible things. Hasn't the happiness of our family been ruined, then?" Kuniko's voice rose. She was trembling.

"Perhaps I exaggerated when I said that man was that 'animal.' But for a man, what comes first is his work. After that, to love women. This is instinct. His way of loving may occasionally have something of the beast in it, but when that is completely denied then I want to say this kind of thing. But of course I don't think that what I've done is good. I feel it's entirely unforgivable towards you. Only, when I consider my side of it alone, I cannot in good conscience blame myself all that much. But I don't by any means think it's good. There's no question it's bad. But my conscience is numbed by the habit."

"You have never said that kind of thing up to now. It's the first time I've heard it."

"Because there was no necessity to say it. And because I'm not too proud of such thoughts."

"In other words, even you think it's a bad thing."

"That may be so."

"If you think it's bad, then from now on you will never do such a thing?"

"I'd like to say so."

"Unless you say so clearly, I won't have any peace of mind."

"Probably that kind of thing won't happen again. I'll do my best to guard against such situations."

"Somehow the way you say that doesn't inspire any trust."

I wanted, for Kuniko's sake as well as my own, to assert positively: "Never." But, feeling as if I were being watched by an honest person inside myself, I could not say it.

"Please put up with things as they are. If you press me too hard, I don't know what I'll say. There's a proverb that the cornered mouse will bite the cat."

"What a terrible mouse."

"Usually in these matters it's the man who is the mouse."

That time, barely, we were able to get to a point where we could laugh together about it. But the blow that this revelation dealt Kuniko was greater than I thought. I regretted having said something that I need not have said. The fact was that without producing any good result it had simply marred Kuniko's consecrated jewel of happiness. Of course, that happiness had been perfect because of a falsehood. But it is a question as to how far a woman can establish her happiness upon the truth, particularly a weak woman like Kuniko.

Perhaps, if I'd realized this a little earlier on, I could have managed things without killing Kuniko. This thought of mine is extremely cynical, but if by means of it I could have managed not to kill a woman, one cannot say that even such a thought is bad.

However, loose as I was in my thoughts, I was strictly faithful. Even Kuniko believed there was none of that kind of thing in my life now.

And so, three or four uneventful years went by. In my work, I'd come to a dead end. Strangely, I no longer had deep feelings about anything. I became incapable of enthusiasm, of throwing myself into something. I would get slightly interested in some material or theme for a play. But as I wrote, it would soon become disagreeable to me. In other words, I could not sustain my interest in the writing. Naturally, I neglected it more and more, but even so, as if remembering to, I would now and then write a one-act play. When I'd written it, people who'd liked my work in the past by force of inertia would graciously praise it, but I myself wasn't happy with it.

There had also been times before when I couldn't write. Back then, I had squarely faced the problem and struggled with it. One time, I'd had an experience that enabled me to write again. So this time, too, I thought it much the same thing and didn't worry too much about it. There was no need to think that a temporary phenomenon was the dead end of my career. Soon, somehow—I even had that kind of optimistic feeling. In the previous instance, something rather important had taken place in my personal life, and my feelings had really been revived. Perhaps this time too something of that kind would arise. Although I was fearful of something happening at home, if some kind of storm wind started blowing through my life, unpleasant though it might be, it would probably get me back on my feet, I thought.

A certain critic, discerning my mental condition in my work, wrote that it would be too bad if I ended up with "the calm of a good-natured man." I felt the same. When I showed the article to Kuniko, she said:

" 'The calm of a good-natured man'? What calm is that? Why can't that critic mind his own business? I don't understand the logic that says household peace and quiet is a problem."

"The Calm of a Good-Natured Man" was a one acter, a collection of sketches of little incidents around the home. When it had been performed, it had been well received in certain quarters. Kuniko knew by hearsay that this critic's domestic arrangements were anything but tranquil, that besides a wife he had a mistress, and besides the mistress another mistress.

"He's not saying I should wreck my domestic harmony. He's warning me that I've gotten too conservative, that I've settled into a feeling that I alone am right. It's too excitable of you to think he's telling me to start sleeping around."

"No, that's certainly what it is. And you agree with him."

"Don't talk like a fool. I'm not about to do anything that somebody else tells me to. Anyway, for you, if your husband doesn't play around, if the children are well and the household is peaceful, it's a perfect life. But for a man, that is not enough. In that sense, I agree with him. The fact is, my feelings of late have become strangely rigid. Somehow I feel enveloped in a drowsy atmosphere where I can move neither hand nor foot. Of course, by force of habit, I've gone on turning things out, but the critic is warning me not to stagnate with such cold, insipid work. He's not telling me to have affairs or anything of the kind. But if you're going to suspect me that way, there's nothing I can do about it. It's outrageous to interpret even my agreeing with him like that."

"You're always talking about your work. But these are the perfect conditions for it. Why can't you work, then? I don't understand that. The children are well, the household is going along nicely, and you have nothing to worry about. These are the best possible conditions for your work, I believe. Aren't you the sort of person who when one of the children catches a little cold, right away you can't get into your work? If the household peace and quiet is broken, *that* is when you wouldn't be able to do your work or anything else."

"That's so. As soon as there are family cares, I become unable to work. That's certainly the case. But what I am saying is something else. It's a real problem. You think there's nothing to find fault with the way things are now. If I raise any objection, you think I'm expecting something unreasonable. It sounds like a complaint, but if you'll allow me to say so, I feel as if this peaceful, uneventful life for the past several years has started to rot me, not that I'm a prize peach or anything. My life has gone bad—what I mean is I've lost the desire to write. You haven't been aware of that, but whenever I've thought I would like to do a little something more in this life of mine, you immediately seem to think that I'm self-indulgently complaining and that I want to enjoy myself more with some other pleasures. So that we're immediately at cross-purposes. What you're thinking and what I'm thinking are completely different."

"I don't know whether they're different or not, but if there's something like what happened before, my feelings immediately go around to that. I know it's a bad habit, but I can't help it."

"You're making all your happiness and unhappiness depend on that one thing. For a woman, that's reasonable enough, but looking at it from my side, I somehow get an unbearable sense of danger."

"And what might that danger be, I wonder? If you will just be a faithful husband, there won't be anything to worry about, will there? The danger is what I'm telling you it is. Even you feel it's dangerous. You have the feeling that sometime or other you're going to make me unhappy because of that. That's why you said that. I may be a fool, but I have a pretty good idea of what's going on."

Kuniko, growing excited, said harsh things unlike her usual self. I too, in the displeasure of being unfairly suspected, began to lose my temper.

"Calm down a little. What you say is like firing real ammunition at an imaginary enemy. It's completely unworthy of you. Even though I'm not taken in by it, if you go on talking like that without understanding my feelings in the slightest, I'll end up getting angry myself."

I didn't think I was angry, but my tone of voice had naturally grown harsh too. Kuniko, becoming quiet, her face suddenly vague, was silent.

The next morning, Kuniko, coming to where I slept, apologized profusely for her scene the night before.

"I understand. I don't think anything of it."

"I'm terribly suspicious. It's because my former circumstances were bad. Last night, after I went to bed, I thought about what I'd said and couldn't forgive myself. Actually, I got up and quietly came to your bedside. You were sound asleep, so I didn't wake you. But it weighed on my mind so I couldn't sleep well."

"How foolish you are. You ought to become a little more easygoing about things. You have the disposition for it."

"When I'm easygoing, I'm easygoing. But about that one thing I just can't be easygoing. It's a defect of mine. I've been used to a very bad environment. When something was bad, I had the strength to accept it as such. But when I think of how happy I am now, I'm completely unable to bear even a little unpleasantness. I'm willful that way. I don't like things left unresolved."

"That's a truly good quality of yours. But I have the feeling that you will blow a little thing up into a great big thing. It makes me uneasy."

"I understand. That's my worst trait, isn't it? I should trust to you in everything and be easy in my mind. Is that it?"

"That will be good."

"My mind's at rest. From now on, I will never have any strange suspicions. I think I'm the happiest woman in the world. You, too, will never do anything to make me worry. That's how things will be."

This meant we were back where we'd started, but it was boring talking about it. I chimed in with her and left it at that.

My third child was born. As usual, the quiet, tedious days went by. Although well aware that my life was going to the bad, I had no one to complain to and naturally turned on Kuniko.

"You must think I'm some kind of domestic animal."

"Why would I think that?"

"At least, you'd like to make me into a domestic animal."

"What makes you think that strange kind of thing?"

"You always speak disparagingly of people like the old man of Yoshizawa who cared about nothing except keeping the family wealth intact, but what you want out of me is not the least bit different. Of course, you don't care about money, but you've simply substituted family happiness for it. In the sense that you're filleting another person to suit your own convenience, it's exactly the same thing."

This sort of false charge that I brought against Kuniko amused even me.

"Do you mean you feel as if you've been filleted for my sake?"

"Yes. I feel as if my backbone had started to rot a little."

"That's an illness called spinal tuberculosis." Kuniko burst out laughing herself.

"That's why unless I treat it quickly it will become something dreadful. It's still not too late. That's why I'm anxious about it."

"If that's so, in other words I'm something like a germ."

"That's exactly right. There's a comic haiku* about the poison brewing medicinal tea in the next room."

"What does that mean?"

"If you don't understand, that's perfect."

Even my accusations, if I brought them off skillfully, ended in laughter like this. But if I got slightly entangled, there were many times when I could not control myself.

The uneventful, peaceful days and months continued to pass. But this uneventful peacefulness, as far as my own feelings were concerned, was anything but uneventful and peaceful. I felt as though I had fallen into a quagmire where, no matter how much I struggled, there was nothing to serve as a foothold and therefore no way out. Everything was hopelessly boring.

I tried such pursuits as hatching goldfish eggs and raising little birds; in the winter, hunched over in my sleeveless work coat, on the sunny veranda, I patched the paper doors; preparing heaps of compost, I planted dahlias and chrysanthemums in the flower beds. My life was no different from that of a retired old man.

From childhood, I had enjoyed doing calligraphy. If asked, I

*In the haiku the master's illness is caused by sexual excess. His concubine, brewing medicinal tea in the next room, is, without knowing it, the source of the disease. (translator's note)

would willingly fill sheets of colored or half-sized paper. Even now, when there was no one to ask, I often rolled back the carpet, spread out the paper and took up my brush. At this rate, I thought, in another five or six years rather than a playwright I'll be a calligrapher.

Kuniko often said that she would never let our daughter be a writer. I agreed with her. Although I don't think that all writers are like myself, once a writer gets into a mental state like mine, he is certainly a menace to family life. Thinking "if it will make me grow," I naturally began to hope for something out of the ordinary to happen. Despite my fine words in the past, I even had fantasies of a love affair that would put me into a frenzy.

When I wrote a woman's part, usually only one woman came to mind. In a play, there would be three or four women characters, yet I could make only one of them come to life. Moreover, this woman was a person who had appeared in all my plays. From a standpoint of craft, I was already tired of the lady. In other words, the fact that finally I knew only one kind of woman was exasperating to me as a writer. The truth was that except for Kuniko I could not create any woman in her totality. Was there ever such a pitiable playwright as myself? At times, even I felt sorry for myself.

At this point, I asked myself just how much of a writer I was.

Some twenty years or so earlier, Shimazaki Toson,* writing *The Broken Commandment* and determined to finish the work no matter what the sacrifice, had drastically retrenched his living expenses. As a result, his family had suffered from malnutrition and several of his daughters, one by one, had starved to death. Reading this, I became extremely angry. I wanted to ask whether *The Broken Commandment* was worth such a price. That several of his children had died on its account was no light matter. Surely it outweighed the question of whether or not *The Broken Commandment* was completed, I thought.

Now, however, regarding myself, no doubt the same thing

*1872–1943 (translator's note)

would be thought by others: "For us, it is of no importance whether a playwright like yourself can or cannot create more than one woman character. Instead we should prefer you to avoid making your one woman the least bit unhappy on that account. Probably it will be as well for you to hatch goldfish eggs. The patching of paper doors, too, will be good. It is a good thing, also, to try to make the dahlias bloom beautifully. And even if you don't labor away mightily at this late hour, there are any number of young playwrights coming along one after the other. Nobody cares whether you've gone to seed like this . . ."

Perhaps, as a disinterested observer, I would have said this too. Since I was the playwright, however, I could not easily think so. A playwright of my quality did not come along often in any period. Although I disliked the word "genius," if a rare and chosen talent was genius, then surely I was the man. I hadn't yet completed the expression of that talent. If I were to end now, something whose destiny it was to be given to the world would be buried forever. I should not be living this kind of life. I was not living up to my destiny. Such were my thoughts.

Nowadays, this kind of belief in the supremacy of art is not popular. But the writers of the past generally thought this way. Shimazaki's *The Broken Commandment* is squarely in that tradition. Precisely because there is this feeling of fanatical devotion in the tenacity that a man brings to his work humanity has been able to advance. Or rather, it is this feeling alone that has caused humanity to advance.

I could not, in the end, know how much of a writer I was. But my feeling was as I have described. Perhaps, though, if this kind of life went on another four or five years, I could not tell what would become even of that feeling. This was where I'd gotten to in my life. But even if this life had continued, and I'd ended as an untalented citizen who never wrote anything, perhaps that would have been for my happiness. After Kuniko's death, I felt this deeply.

For the first time in a long time, one of my plays—at that, an old play I had half forgotten—was to be performed by a certain troupe. If it was all the same, I said, I would prefer it to be something in which I had a little more confidence. But there were the actors' wishes to be considered, and I was asked by all means to let it be this play. I had no choice but to say yes. I read the play over with the feeling that I was looking at somebody else's work. But while there were passages that seemed unbearably immature, on the other hand there were places where I had truly taken pleasure in the writing. They possessed a charm which I was now wholly incapable of, I thought. I thought that to be able to have a genuine interest in the work itself was truly a thing to be thankful for. To me as I was now, that charm, that savor was entirely lost. No matter what I wrote, I almost immediately thought it was trivial. I could not go on with it. But that play, although extremely immature both in subject and technique, had been written by an author in real earnest, convinced that it was an extraordinary masterpiece. One could say it was laughable, but when I looked back on it from the present, when I had lost that feeling, I felt a longing for the past.

As a matter of course, frequent invitations came from the theater to attend rehearsals, but I felt no desire to go. I left the play on its own. One evening, two or three days before the play opened, I suddenly had a visit from an actress named Asama Yukiko. She talked about such things as how to perform her role, but I had nothing to say.

"She's a very simple woman, isn't she? The most frequent type in Japan. Or doesn't that type exist any more among you ladies? Don't tell me she's become a relic of the last century."

". . ." The actress drew in her shoulders and laughed.

"In your eyes, such a woman may seem like an antique. If that's so, the hero also may belong in an antique shop . . ."

"The hero is yourself, isn't he?"

"No. I'm not that kind of person."

"Liar. Mr. Sasayama is modelling the role on you."

"That's a dirty trick. I'm not going to see the play, of course, but he should lay off such mischief."

"It's not necessarily mischief. Unless there's some kind of source, the interpretation becomes terribly arbitrary. First of all, your mannerisms show up in the speeches. I thought that when I met you."

"It's bad taste to make the role a caricature of the author. I'm not going to stop you at this late hour, but from now on, when I agree to a performance, I'll attach a condition that you are not to do that kind of thing."

"I'm in trouble, then."

"How is that?"

"Because it leaves me in a quandary."

"Try telling me about it."

"Actually, I came to meet your wife."

"Ah, so?" I smiled. "That's even worse. Right now she seems to be putting the children to bed, but if that's what you've come for, I won't let you see her."

"Oh, what shall I do, then?"

"How could you even think of such a thing?"

"Really, just a minute will be enough. I've heard that she's extremely beautiful . . ."

"Ha ha."

"Please, Master. I beg of you." The actress spoke with a coaxing look.

"By the by, are your parents in health?"

"No."

"What about your aunts?"

"Aunts? I have three aunts in all."

"Well then, make one of them your model. That will do nicely."

"Maa! You awful man!"

"For the kind of woman in my plays, that's enough. It's a rude comment on your aunt, but . . ."

"I can't possibly see her in time," the actress pouted.

"You're a fool. My wife would have been very interested to meet an actress, and even though she said nothing she would have come out. But now that you've said that kind of thing, she won't."

"But she still doesn't know anything of this, does she?"

"She sleeps in the room across the corridor. She's heard everything."

"How unpleasant. You're very unkind." The actress laughed loudly. Kuniko must be making a bitter face, I thought. She must be thinking bitter thoughts of me, having this easy, laughing conversation with a young woman. At the thought, I felt ashamed. I should have conducted this meeting from the start with a somewhat more dignified attitude, I thought regretfully.

When I was silent, the actress, having evidently given up her hope of meeting Kuniko, said:

"Why don't you ever come to rehearsals, Master?"

"Because it would displease me to see them."

". . . You think that you wouldn't care for our acting methods."

"There's that, but more than that I don't have any interest in that script."

"I think it's a very good play."

"If you're impressed by that kind of thing, there's nothing I can do about it."

"Yes. Even if there's nothing to be done about it I think it's a good play."

The actress repeatedly urged me to come see the dress rehearsal the next day. If she was to be disappointed in the one hope, I must please at least agree to this.

"When does it start?"

"At ten o'clock."

"That's in the morning."

"Yes."

"Well, I'll be there by then."

"Be sure to, now. Thank you very much."

"Not at all."

Suddenly lowering her voice, the actress whispered: "Bring your wife too." With a mischievous look, she stuck out the tip of her tongue.

Shortly afterward, the actress went back in the rickshaw she had kept waiting. If I were a novelist, I would probably have to describe in detail the relationship which followed with this actress. Perhaps I should write about it even though I'm not a novelist, but I have neither the interest nor the perseverance to do so. At any rate, some time afterward, I became infatuated with her. Whether or not I was truly in love with her, I can't really say myself, but, anyway, I was infatuated.

As for Asama Yukiko, she was most certainly not in love with me. If one were to ask why, despite that, she approached me in that way, it was because she wanted to become known by having an affair with me. Another reason was that she desired by such means to break off with the young man, younger even than herself, whom she'd been living with up to then. I was obliged to pay off all of the several months' worth of debts and back rent the two had accumulated. Because of the loans they had jointly signed for, the pair, although quarrelling every day, had been unable to part from each other.

I was told that the young man had departed, so one day I went to her house. It was in such a mess that one wondered whether this was indeed a human habitation. There was not a single thing there that simply served its purpose. In the brazier, there were not only cigarette butts, but fruit peelings, movie programs, pencil shavings, and fragments of a coffee cup. There was little to choose between it and a garbage dump. By way of bedclothes, there was a filthy coverlet with its velvet border gone, and a single "priest's pillow" with a towel wrapped around it and buckwheat chaff trickling from a burst seam. The chipped lampshade, the burn marks on the tatami, the unwashed dishes and bowls and cups—everything was in indescribably bad order.

"You mean you've actually been able to live in this place?"

"Yes. That's why I've never been able to feel at home here."

"No wonder. It's like a mouse-hole, or a den of foxes and badgers."

"There are fleas. I just can't stand it."

"The thing is what to do about it."

"I'd like to set fire to it and burn it down."

"This is no time for jokes."

When I started along the dark corridor toward the kitchen, I kicked some light object. It rolled all the way into the privy, the door of which had been left open.

"I kicked something."

"What?"

"I don't know what it was, but it rolled into the privy."

Yukiko got up and went into the privy.

"Oh dear, isn't that my hat?"

I burst out laughing. "But you probably don't wear it any more."

"I just bought it. Oh, this is terrible."

Saying this kind of thing, Yukiko retrieved the hat from a damp part of the funnel-shaped urinal. After sniffing it briefly, she announced: "Disinfection by sunlight." Finding a sunny spot in the garden, she hung the hat up on a tree.

"My god, the things you do. You should set fire to that hat and burn it. It's all dirty, isn't it?"

"No. This hat becomes me the best."

Recalling this incident half a year later, I felt keenly that indeed that hat had suited her head the best. Truth to tell, however, in matters of that sort, as I knew only too well at the time, I was completely at Yukiko's mercy.

When the troupe to which she belonged was making a tour of the provinces, Yukiko would often try to summon me to whatever town they were in, but I never answered. I was very much afraid of this affair being found out by Kuniko. Luckily, the people around me were well aware of my fear, and I also kept a nervous eye on the gossip columns in the theater section of the newspapers. For three or four months, Kuniko knew nothing of our affair.

One day, however, it suddenly appeared, complete with photograph, as a human interest story. For Yukiko, this accomplished perfectly her two goals, but I was momentarily somewhat flustered. Taking advantage of Kuniko's apparently not having seen it yet, I immediately took the newspaper to my study and hid it there. Probably that will do, I thought. Even a newspaper, once it has published something like this, won't run the damn thing again. And certainly no reporter would be fool enough to deliberately come and ask for an interview with my wife. I felt more or less reassured. But all that day, I had a bad feeling of being unable to lift up my head before Kuniko.

The next day, however, our maid heard about it from somebody in the neighborhood and told Kuniko. So everything ended in failure.

It was strange to me why a newspaper would report such a trivial matter as whether or not a person like myself was having an affair with an actress like Yukiko. Although Kuniko suffered a great deal, I wasn't particularly bothered by being exposed this way. Recently, however, a certain poet had had his affair with a truant young woman—probably even more truant than Yukiko—written up in a newspaper on the eve of his departure for Europe. Although it was another person's affair, I was terribly angry. What displeased me was the cruelty of the reporter who had chosen to publish his revelation in the evening edition of the day before the departure. Anyone who knows what the day before a departure is for the family and friends would never be able to do such a thing. If it was something that had to be published, why not publish it after the departure? When I thought of the reporter's triumph at having timed the article to coincide with the departure, I felt bitterly the truth of the adage: "There is no medicine you can give a fool." No doubt what the poet had done, the same as my affair with Yukiko, was nothing praiseworthy. Still, the girl was that kind of girl. It was not as if he'd trifled with the affections of a fastidious young virgin. Wasn't she just fifty or a hundred steps away from being an unlicensed prostitute? It was the reporter's behavior, in publishing such an article at a time when in every sense it would have the most effect, that is, the day before the departure, that I thought despicable beyond measure. It was atrociously cruel treatment of the feelings of a person who was leaving his wife and child for a while and going overseas.

On the morning of his departure, I heard from friends who went to see him off, the poet's eyes were bloodshot as if he'd been crying all night. Since he was a man who *always* looked as if he'd been crying all night, I didn't set any store by that. But I sympathized with his misfortune. Soon afterward, however, when I saw this poet's reports from Russia in that same newspaper, I again thought it strange.

Be that as it may, in my case, I didn't actually care about the article's appearance. And although she said things that indicated great consternation, since it was what she'd hoped for Yukiko on the contrary seemed happy about it. Actresses such as Yukiko, unless this sort of thing happens, are not women who will attract much attention either by their looks or their art. When I say this, it sounds as though I were famous; but when one has been writing for more than twenty years, little by little one becomes better known than an Asama Yukiko. For Yukiko, it was enough if she merely linked her name with mine. Be it either ill repute or ridicule, if she could publicize herself by such means her desire would be fulfilled. So the one who drew the loser's ticket in all this was Kuniko.

"I'm not going to say any more about it. I just have the feeling that everything up to now has been like a dream. When I think that none of what I believed in was true, I feel as if I alone were a peculiar person. It's so lonely, I can't bear it. In a word, I've been a fool. I went ahead and thought everything was beautiful. I thought it was true. I can only think that I was a very great fool."

"You always think about that one thing, and so it's a problem. To judge from your words, you've made up your mind that truth no longer exists in this world . . ."

"Wait a moment. I more or less understand what you're saying. That's all very well. It's dangerous to believe as I do that everything depends on that alone. And there are many other kinds of truth. I understand that. But in my position, there is absolutely no room to think of things separately, as this is this and that is that. You're a clever person, and I'm a fool. When I listen to you, things are turned into their opposites. But to tell you the truth, I always have the feeling afterward that I've been tricked by you again. To think that of a person whom one considers to be more remarkable than anyone else is not a pleasant thing at all. But I just can't help thinking it. What can I do? It is this feeling that I alone am unlike everyone else that's the most unbearably lonely."

"If you're going to talk like that, there's nothing I can say."

"I don't know how this matter will turn out either, but when I think that from now on this kind of thing will be happening for the rest of my life, somehow I feel as though the future had turned into pitch darkness."

"There were reasons, but certainly just by making you have such feelings what I did is wrong. It's strange to say this to you, but from the beginning I've only thought of women like Yukiko as lead. Why a man who has gold or silver in his possession should also lust after lead is beyond my ability to explain. But unless you believe at least this much, I won't feel right myself. You must believe that if you were the silver, I never thought of Yukiko as anything more than the lead. I recognize that what I did was bad. At the same time, please believe that from the start my feelings were only of that degree."

"In that case, what do you intend to do about that actress?"

"Break with her. If she's in the newspapers, as an actress she's accomplished her purpose."

"What are your own feelings?"

"H'm."

"What are they?"

"To speak honestly, there may be a little regret. But parting from her won't be any great hardship."

"Won't it be a little painful?"

"I can't tell. I won't know until the time comes."

"And so perhaps you won't be able to leave her?"

"No. I'm certainly going to break with her. But you asked what my feelings were, so I told you."

"And if you feel that way indefinitely, what then?"

"That won't happen. All I thought was that at the time there might be some lingering regret."

I felt it was strange how things changed when I was thinking about them by myself and when I was talking about them with Kuniko. My relationship with Yukiko, which when I thought about it alone was a lighthearted nothing, when I talked about it with Kuniko became a terribly difficult, burdensome matter. Although on second thought that was only to be expected, it was strange how I felt things change their meaning. I decided to break immediately with Yukiko. Giving her enough money to live on for a year, I settled the affair easily.

This is something I hesitate to write about, and furthermore feel ashamed of for myself, but by my relationship with Yukiko I felt a sort of new life. It is a fact that in the quagmire where I'd been struggling these past four or five years without being able to escape, that affair gave me a small foothold. My thoughts turned to my work; my interest in it was reborn. In general, I felt as if I'd been liberated from the life in which I had been strangely imprisoned until then. I finally got back to my work. Not letting this opportunity slip, I resolved to write the somewhat ambitious drama that I had been thinking of.

It was a period play, to be called *The Lord of Tsukiyama*, and it was no easy task just to research the historical facts. In the story itself, there was an interest that could be seen as inherently dramatic. Although the Lord of Tsukiyama lacked the showy brilliance of a Yodogimi, there was a dormant, weird, brutal feeling about him. The morbid, strangely sensational character of his son Nobuyasu, if the part was well written, would be interesting also. The enmity of Sakai Tadatsugu towards Nobuyasu, the affection of Ieyasu for Nobuyasu, after that the relationship of Nobunaga and Ieyasu, the secret understanding between the Lord of Tsukiyama and Katsuyori, the character of Genkei, the Chinese doctor, and the plot with its various complications—if I could skillfully pull it all together, although not particularly modern in feeling, it promised to be a powerful full-length play.

I desired, now, to write something, of which I could think: at least I did my work. And so I completely immersed myself in the play. This had been a very rare thing for me of late.

I was able to forget Yukiko unexpectedly quickly. Just a month before, she had been Yukiko whom I could not forget for a single day; now she was purely and simply a woman of my past. It was not only Yukiko. To Kuniko also, and the children, I was able to be indifferent in the same way. This was a good thing, I thought. In addition, I'm sorry to say, my feelings became extraordinarily distant from the goldfish, the little birds, and the dahlias. I was in my study from morning on. When I'd taken a brief walk in the afternoon, I shut myself in the study again until I went to bed. I was with my family only at meals, and at such times my humor was by no means good. When the children were noisy I often shouted at them, and when Kuniko brought up household matters I would get angry and not answer her.

I was constantly excited. Especially when I was writing the part of Nobuyasu, I felt partially possessed by his strangely fretful rages. As I tried to experience his feelings and convey his frenzy, as when he cursed a dancer's incompetence and took his bow and arrow and shot her, or when, encountering a priest while out hawking, he blamed him for the day's poor take and, tying a rope around his neck, spurred the horse to drag him to his death, I naturally became a little strange myself. From fatigue, I also became easily agitated.

Kuniko, already defeated just by the matter of Yukiko, was evidently unable to bear this new mental condition of mine. Every day, with her lonely face, and yet nervously careful not to let the children get in the way of my work, she was a pathetic figure. At times, even that cowering figure made me lose my temper.

"How would it be if you were a little more lively? Just because I get excited, there's no need to be all nervous and timid. The atmosphere of this house is gloomy and disagreeable. It's curious how when I come out of the doldrums you hold back. Cheer up a little. When I say I want some quiet, you don't have to go around in fear and trembling."

"I've just lost all my self-confidence. If I say this sort of thing, perhaps I'll be scolded again, but I've lost my bearings in this house. I don't know what I should do. Up until now, I've felt that the family was all one, somehow, but lately I've had the unbearably lonely sense that we're all oddly separate—you are you, I am I, the children are the children. What has happened? Perhaps I'm having a nervous breakdown."

"Just when I've gotten some energy back, it's a nuisance to have you say that kind of thing. I can't be bothered with that kind of thing. Isn't it good that I am I and you are you? It's only to be expected that when I'm immersed in my work you aren't able to be with me. If you go on as usual, that will be good. When you put on that strangely depressed face, I get angry just as much as I get excited."

"I'm happy too that you've become absorbed in your work. But although it would be good if this were so without anything else, there's just been one unpleasant thing after another. I'm somewhat floored by it all. It would be good if it were, once our feelings had completely healed, but somehow I feel as if it weren't over . . ."

"It might be good for you if our feelings were the way you want them, but I don't want them that way now. I feel remote from such things. Why won't you leave me alone? In your feelings, you come following me everywhere. There's no point in your pursuing my feelings where they are now. Nothing says that any couple have to be together in their feelings all the time. Katsumi Nori, now, was a Japanese of the old school. When he took ship for America, he told his wife he was just going to see someone off and went all the way to America. He wasn't acting on a whim, either. Back in those days, a sea voyage was a perilous affair. He did the right thing. You, too, when I'm intent on my work, have enough margin in yourself not to meddle with my feelings. It's incredibly annoying."

"In other words, I'm a hindrance to your work."

"That's right. Or rather than you being the hindrance, your feelings that keep coming after me without understanding anything are the hindrance. I don't understand why you have to cling to my feelings when I'm working."

"I don't think I've interfered the least little bit with your work."

"That's what you think, but it comes to the same thing. Be more unconcerned, will you? Unconcerned. If you will be lighthearted in your feelings, then I can devote myself with an easy mind to my work. You're following me all over the place. I can't take it any longer."

"I don't really understand what you say at all. I don't feel as if I've clung to you the least little bit. But now that you say I have, I feel as if I had too. And seeing that of late I've been absolutely unable to feel lighthearted, perhaps what you say is true. Even so, what shall I do? And even if I understand for a while, I don't have the least bit of faith that I can become like that."

"Don't bother me any more. You are you. Do whatever you want. I am I. I don't want to negotiate with you on the basis of that kind of feeling. If you do it a little more, I'm going off somewhere to be alone and do my work. I'm not Katsumi, but I might just tell you I was going for a walk and not come back for six months or a year. That would be good."

My patience gone, I looked right at Kuniko with eyes full of malevolence as I said this. I really thought it would be good.

". . ." Her face going slightly pale, Kuniko silently gazed into my face.

"I just don't understand. I seem to understand, but I don't."

"If you don't understand, you don't understand. Fine."

It was an evening four or five days after we'd had this kind of talk. Until then, there had been nothing particularly strange about Kuniko's behavior. Her sad and lonely air was the same, but she seemed somewhat calmer than before. I avoided as much as I could any exchange of feelings. That night also, I was working in my second-floor study. I was aware that downstairs, unable to sleep from some time before, Kuniko was now and again getting up, going to the privy, opening the clothes closet or going off toward the kitchen. Although it was already two in the morning, and I wondered what she was doing, I did not call down to her. Soon, though, it became quiet. Probably she's gone to sleep, I thought. Then, I couldn't tell how many minutes later, I suddenly heard footsteps on the ladder-stairs, *mishiri, mishiri*, as if someone were climbing with extreme stealth. It's Kuniko, I thought, but I didn't want the kind of argument we'd had before. My voice deliberately loud, I called out:

"Who is it?" There was no answer, but that same climbing sound: *mishiri, mishiri*. I silently continued writing. Even when the door slid open, I did not turn around.

"I don't want to talk right now." Saying this, I only then looked at Kuniko. Both hands clutching at the thick paper doors, Kuniko stood up in the foot-long opening. Her face gave me a shock. It was a death-face—Kuniko's face was certainly not of this world. Her mouth like an upside down flattened V, she stared at me through narrowed, but completely unfocused eyes. I felt Kuniko had done something irretrievable. When I got up and went to her, she abruptly toppled forward from between the doors and clung to me.

"What damn fool thing have you done!" I was shaking with excitement and anger.

Kuniko, her eyes closed, clung to me with her whole body.

Unable to stand, I sank to a sitting position with Kuniko in my arms. Two or three times, she started to cough something up.

"What did you take? What did you take?"

Kuniko, her face buried in my bosom, vomited something. I pulled her away from me. Some crystals of what seemed to be mercuric chloride were mixed in with her vomit. Kuniko still held me hard around my waist. Unclasping her hands, I ran downstairs and got the maids up. One I sent immediately for the doctor, telling her to say that Kuniko had swallowed mercuric chloride, that she'd vomited just two crystals, that I couldn't tell how much else she'd swallowed and that her condition was already very bad.

By the time I'd gotten back upstairs, Kuniko had gone dead pale. Undulating her body left and right, she was moaning.

"Kuniko. Kuniko." Already Kuniko seemed beyond help. Calling the maid, I tried to make Kuniko drink some water, but it was no good.

Kuniko suffered agony. When the doctor had come, and was making preparations to pump her stomach, Kuniko finally drew her last breath.

✲

✲

A Gray Moon

✲

As I stood in the roofless corridor of Tokyo Station, the air was still but chilly. The light overcoat I was wearing was just warm enough. My two friends having taken the Ueno train which had come in first, I was waiting alone for the Shinagawa train.

From a thinly clouded sky, a gray moon shone weakly upon the fire ruins of Nihonbashi. Perhaps ten days old, the moon was low and somehow seemed close at hand. Although it was only eight-thirty, there were not many people about. The wide, deserted corridor seemed all the wider for its emptiness.

The headlights of the train appeared far in the distance. After a while, it came swiftly sliding into the station. It was not crowded, and I was able to get a seat across the aisle and near a door. On my right was a woman of about fifty, in baggy work trousers. On my left, a boy of sixteen or seventeen who seemed to be a factory worker sat with his back to me. He was sideways to the door, with his legs over the end of the seat where the armrest should have been. I had glanced at the boy's face when I'd gotten on. His eyes were closed, his jaw hung slackly open, and the upper part of his body was slowly swaying back and forth. Or rather, he was slumping forward, pulling himself up, and slumping forward again, repeating the same movement over and over. There was something unpleasant about such motions continued even in sleep. I left just enough space between the boy and myself so that I would not seem to be avoiding him.

At Yuraku-cho and Shimbashi, the train began to fill up. Several passengers seemed to be on their way back from food-hunting expeditions. A ruddy, round-faced man of twenty-five or -six lowered his outsize knapsack to the seat between me and the boy, then stood straddling it. Behind him a middle-aged man, also with a knapsack on his back, was being pushed off his feet by the press of people. Looking at the young man in front of him, he said:

"You don't mind if I put this down?" Not waiting for an answer, he began to slip the pack from his shoulders.

"Wait a minute." The young man turned around, as if to defend his own knapsack. "There isn't room for two."

"Oh. Excuse me." The man glanced up at the baggage rack, but there didn't seem to be room there either. Twisting his body in the cramped space, he worked the pack back onto his shoulders.

Apparently having a change of heart, the young man told him that if he wanted to he could rest his pack on the seat.

"It's all right. Mine isn't that heavy. It would only be in the way. I thought I'd set it down a while, but it doesn't matter." The older man nodded his thanks for the offer.

It made me feel good to have seen this. I thought to myself that people's feelings had truly changed from the way they had been.

At Hamamatsu-cho and then Shinagawa, some riders got off but more got on. Even among these new and more numerous passengers, the boy continued to fall forward and catch himself as before.

"Just take a look at the face on him," a man's voice said. The man was one of a group of four or five office workers. The others burst into laughter. From where I sat I could not see the boy's face. But the man had a funny way of speaking, and probably the boy did have an odd expression. An atmosphere of good humor began to prevail in the crowded car.

Just then, the round-faced man turned to the man behind him. Tapping his stomach with his forefinger, he said in a low voice:

"That boy's just this side of starvation."

Seeming somewhat surprised, the other man looked silently at the boy.

Even the men who had laughed now seemed to think that something might be wrong with the boy.

"Is he sick?" one asked.

"Drunk, more likely," another one said. But then someone else said:

"No, it's not that." Perhaps having sensed what it was, the men were suddenly quiet.

There was a tear in the shoulder of the boy's coarsely woven factory uniform. It had been patched from the inside with a scrap of towel-cloth. Beneath the visor of the army forage cap which he had on backwards, the boy's slender, dirty nape looked forlorn. He was no longer swaying back and forth. He was rubbing his cheek against a strip of paneling between the door and the window. Like a child, he had made the piece of wood into a person in his fatigue, and was trying to snuggle up to it.

"Hey." A big man standing in front of the boy placed his hand on his shoulder. "Where are you going?"

At first, the boy did not answer. When the question was repeated, he said in a dead-tired voice:

"I'm going to Ueno."

"No, you're not. You're headed in exactly the wrong direction. This train goes to Shibuya."

The boy got to his feet and started to look out the window. Abruptly, he lost his balance and was thrown lightly against me by the forward motion of the car. Caught unawares, I did something which I could not comprehend afterwards. Almost as if by a reflex action, I thrust the boy away from me with my shoulder. It was an act that was such a betrayal of what I really felt that I was shocked at myself. I was all the more sorry and ashamed because the resistance of the boy's body against mine had been extremely slight. My own weight was down to a hundred and ten in those days. But the boy must have weighed far less than that.

I tried saying from behind the boy:

"You should have changed at Tokyo Station. Where did you get on?"

"At Shibuya," the boy answered. He did not turn around. Someone else said:

"Well then, you're coming full circle."

Pressing his forehead to the window, the boy peered out at the darkness. Then, giving it up, he murmured so that I could hardly hear him:

"It makes no difference."

The boy's words, spoken only to himself, stayed with me long afterwards.

The passengers around him didn't concern themselves further with the boy. Probably they thought there was nothing they could do for him. I myself felt that as things were there was nothing I could do either. If I'd had some food with me, I might have given that to him for my own peace of mind. Money might have been no help to him even in the daytime. At nine o'clock at night, there was still less hope of his being able to buy any food.

With the same gloomy emotion, I got off at Shibuya.

This incident took place on October 16, 1945.

Design by David Bullen
Typeset in Mergenthaler Electra
by Wilsted & Taylor
Printed by Haddon Craftsmen
on acid-free paper